E. Wordsworth

Short Words for Long Evenings

E. Wordsworth

Short Words for Long Evenings

Reprint of the original, first published in 1875.

1st Edition 2024 | ISBN: 978-3-38525-129-8

Verlag (Publisher): Outlook Verlag GmbH, Zeilweg 44, 60439 Frankfurt, Deutschland
Vertretungsberechtigt (Authorized to represent): E. Roepke, Zeilweg 44, 60439 Frankfurt, Deutschland
Druck (Print): Books on Demand GmbH, In de Tarpen 42, 22848 Norderstedt, Deutschland

SHORT WORDS

FOR

LONG EVENINGS.

BY

E. WORDSWORTH,

Author of " Thoughts for the Chimney Corner."

Or, if the air will not permit,
Some still, removéd place will fit,
Where glowing embers through the robin,
Teach light to counterfeit a gloom ;
Far from all resort of mirth,
Save the cricket on the hearth,
Or the bellman's drowsy charm
To bless the doors from nightly harm.

MILTON.

LONDON:

HATCHARDS, 187 PICCADILLY.

1875.

PREFACE.

Some of the readers of the "Chimney Corner" having kindly expressed a wish for a few more papers in the same style, the present little volume has been written, the object being, as before, to furnish those who have few opportunities for quiet thought apart from their daily life, with something that may remind them *in* and *by* the very life they live, the tools they habitually use, and the circumstances that commonly surround them, of the unseen, the permanent, and the divine. One or two of the present series will, perhaps, be found too difficult for the very poor in our agricultural parishes. The writer has had no opportunity of trying the experiment. Perhaps the class just above the poorest would not find them so. Speculative difficulties will occur to persons of a certain cast of mind, whether they have had the benefits of what is called "education" or not; it seems to be in the nature of things, for thinkers, as well as poets, are born—not made.

As on a previous occasion, selections of Hymns, and texts of Scripture, have been added. Perhaps any one in the habit of holding mothers' meetings, or other gatherings of a similar kind, would be able, by a little preparation beforehand, to present the thoughts thus grouped together in a more intelligible form than could be done by a mere hasty reading of portions of Scripture.

A few words of comment from the reader or speaker, (whose familiarity with the listeners' faces will soon discover when they have grasped an idea and when they have not,) will often be able to supply some little link, some trifling explanation of a 'hard word,' some missing clue for the elucidation of a difficulty which could not have been anticipated by the author. To the kind offices of such, and with sincere wishes and prayers for the success of all their good endeavours, the following pages are now commended.

St. Matthew's Day,

1874.

CONTENTS.

It will be seen that Nos. 1 and 4 have no Scripture references assigned to them, as the transition seemed too abrupt, owing to the less serious character of the papers.

SHORT WORDS FOR LONG EVENINGS.

I.

BLINKERS.

PEOPLE have often amused themselves with fancying what descriptions a foreigner or a savage would give of this country if he happened to come to it from another whose customs were very unlike our own. Great fun used to be made of the wigs and powder, the paint, patches and hoops of our forefathers and fore-mothers, (if we may use such a word,) and in latter times there have been many jokes about other fashions just as laughable, or seeming as absurd, as these. But there is one curious practice which, as far as I recollect, has never been touched on in stories of this sort. We might fancy a wild man describing our carriages and horses somewhat as follows :—

B

"These English people," he might be made to say, "go about in houses on wheels, fitted up almost like beds, and indeed, as I think, intended for that purpose, for I constantly see persons asleep in them. These houses move wherever they are drawn, by long-haired monsters with four legs. Wonderful creatures are they—fire may be seen flashing from the stones struck by their feet, their breath is like the smoke of a furnace, and their speed swift as that of a bird, and their noise as the roll of thunder. My notion is that the English are afraid of the glance of their eyes, for most commonly there is a kind of black covering placed over them, so that the eye is scarcely to be seen. And indeed, from the terrible size and great power of these monsters, one may easily imagine that their eyes would dart forth flashes hurtful as the lightning, Doubtless the English, who are a wise nation. have some good reason for what they do, but I could not understand their language well enough to learn what it was."

This perhaps is the way an old-fashioned New Zealander, (who had never seen any four-footed creature at his own home, but a rat or a pig,) might be supposed to talk of us and our horses, and that odd custom we have of putting them into blinkers. It does seem a rather ridiculous one certainly; and that draught horses should be half blinded in this way, while saddle horses are allowed the full use of their eyes, has always appeared to me hard, to say the least of it. However I know I am getting out of my depth on this difficult subject, so I will leave the poor horses to their fate, and only ask why *we*, who might have the free use of our eyes if we chose, should so often go about in blinkers, quite as thick and quite as effectual as those to be found on any horse's head, or hung up in any harness-room in the kingdom.

Do we not? In other words do we not often, instead of looking well all round us before we take a step, only fix our eyes on the little point of space exactly before our noses, and never give a thought to anything beyond?

Of course it saves trouble. It is much easier to allow ourselves to be taken up with one idea than to give fair play to half-a-dozen. Far easier to let one feeling, perhaps a good one in itself, guide us, one might say, "run away with us," than to let everything have its due share of attention. But if we do this, let us remember that we are very little better or more intelligent than carriage horses, and not as they are, helpful, but rather a hindrance to the progress of good about us.

This will be made clearer by one or two examples. And here, perhaps, we may ask women especially, to take notice of what follows. For they are, on the whole, very much more taken possession of by some ideas and feelings at least than men. About the commonest pair of blinkers that a woman has put over her eyes, is the temptation to care for one person so much that she is not just to any one else. Perhaps it is the youngest baby. Do we not know mothers who let that youngest baby be a tyrant over themselves and over the whole house? No one must talk—baby is going to sleep. The other children must not have such and such a plaything—baby wants it. She couldn't iron her husband's shirts because baby was so fretful and would not be good with any one else.

All spoilt children may be said to be so, because their fathers and mothers wore a pair of these curious blinkers, that made them shut their eyes to their children's faults.

Well then, there is the economical pair of blinkers. A woman has very rightly been impressed with the truth that a penny saved is a penny got. Quite so, but if she only looks at this one thing she will be sure to make some serious mistakes. She will do what a poor man once very cleverly called, "stepping over twopence to pick up a penny." She will save in shoes, and spend in remedies for broken chilblains. She will grudge a delicate girl a bit of new flannel for her chest, or a slice of meat, and have to spend five or six times as much in doctor's stuff. She will save in a pennyworth of nails, and spend in a long bill from the carpenter. And all this comes of the economical pair of blinkers, not looking fairly at things all round.

Then there is a very blinding pair of blinkers, worse than any of the others, and on it is written, "MY RIGHTS." If we once get possessed by this notion of our rights we shall go on blundering to the end of our lives.

If we are rich we shall go to law about an insignificant slip of land, and spend the value of the land many times over before we have done.

If we are poor we shall fancy some one has affronted us, and lose all the advantages of a good neighbour through a foolish bit of pique.

If we belong to what are called the "middle classes," ten to one we shall have a dispute with somebody about our seat in church, and lose all the good church-going would do us, because we do not get what we consider "our rights." Can such people ever have read the Sermon on the Mount?

Very closely allied to this is the desire we may have to be revenged of some one.*

If we once allow the desire for revenge to take possession of us, we become blind to everything else. We seem driven on, almost forced upon a course which appears to others as mad and unreasonable as it would to ourselves at any other time. Indeed, any strong passion may be said to act like a pair of blinkers, shutting out all right reason, fair play, and calm judgment, only there is not the coachman's hand on the reins to keep the poor horse from going wrong. Love of money, of course does this, so does jealousy, so does self-conceit, and so do many other bad feelings, or even good feelings overstrained and exaggerated.

Suppose, for instance, a father who has lost one very dear child, or a widow or any one else who has had to part with their dearest. Are

---

* Some of us will remember Shylock the Jew, in the "Merchant of Venice." He had one idea—only one, in his mind, "justice and his bond." Portia's speech is the most perfect antidote to this hard, narrow, unchristian spirit. Readers of modern fiction will remember at least *one* instance of the same kind, perhaps many.

they not sometimes a little hard on the survivors?
Do they not feel as if they would like to copy
that old king whose son was drowned at sea,
and who, the song tells us, "never smiled again?"
There is something very attractive to such persons in the idea of "nursing their grief," as we
call it. They have a kind of pleasure in dwelling
on past days, in treasuring up old letters, and
other keepsakes, in going the same walks, in
reading the same books, in dreaming the old
dreams in every possible way. Their eyes can
only look in one direction. They forget that the
living want their thoughts, their sympathy, aye,
their cheerfulness and brightness. It is far less
trouble to go on and on, dwelling beneath the
shadow of a great grief, than to try and take up
fresh interests for the sake of others. But who
mourn most rightly and wisely, they who shut
themselves up in their own selfish sorrow, having
everything dismal and gloomy about them, the
deepest crape, the broadest black-edged paper,
reading nothing but the most melancholy books,
and speaking in the most dreary tones of voice,
or those who try to do what their dead husband,
wife, or friend would have cared for, and to be
what he would like to have seen them, cheerful,
as Christians who hope to meet again hereafter

must ever be! Who throw open their houses
and their hearts to their children and friends; who
mix moderately and reasonably with the world,
however great the effort may be at first, who
spend their time not in bemoaning themselves,
but in trying to make others better and happier?
Believe me, grief is, or may be made, quite as
selfish a thing as joy.

To turn to a lighter subject—Good manners.
Nearly all the rudeness in the world comes from
these blinkers in which so many of our heads
unfortunately find themselves. We don't *want*
to be rude, but our way of looking at life is so
narrow, that we are always saying and doing
awkward things. We go by stiff rules, without
taking grand general views. A true gentleman
or lady (and there are such in all ranks, of
nature's making) looks all round him or her,
and is not merely like the carriage-horse, who
can only just see beyond its own nose.

For instance, there is an old story of a man
having a poor relation at dinner with him. The
mistress of the house seeing there was a bit of
pudding left when every one had been helped,
pressed the poor relation to have it. "Take it,
do, Mr. Smith, for *you* don't get pudding every
day." It was very good natured of her to wish

him to have the pudding, but she took all the plums out of it by her awkward speech, reminding him he was after all but a poor and needy relation. That woman you may be sure generally went about in blinkers.

One other very old story so well illustrates this, that I must tell it yet once more. Louis XIV., of France, told his courtiers, "Ah, you think yourselves very fine gentlemen, but there is an Englishman here who is a better bred man than any of you." They, of course, would not believe it, but not long afterwards the king was going out for a drive, and this English nobleman, Lord Stair, was of the party. "Be so good as to get into my carriage," said the king to one of the Frenchmen. "What, sire, before your majesty? Nothing should induce me to do anything so ill-mannered." "My Lord Stair, will *you* then, be good enough to get into my carriage?" said the king. "Your majesty's commands must always be obeyed," said Lord Stair, and he at once entered the carriage. "There," said the king to his courtiers. "There is an instance of real good breeding. You all chose to place a piece of mere formal etiquette before my express wishes. Lord Stair rose above the letter, and entered into the spirit of good manners. He is without doubt the most finished gentleman of my court." *

And now, as the reader will doubtless be able to comment on this story for himself, I will not spoil it by any additional remarks, or perhaps, I too should be justly accused of wearing blinkers, or in other words, of not knowing when people have had "too much of a good thing."

* This story is given from memory, and the writer would be very glad to know where it is originally told, and whether the present version is correct.

II.

AN OLD CHEST.*

———

THERE was once a Duke and Duchess who had a beautiful estate in France, and a grand house. The duke, from being a common soldier, had risen by his bravery to high rank and wealth; but neither he nor his duchess had ever been made proud and hard-hearted by it, as is sometimes the way with people who have suddenly and unexpectedly become great. Their house was full of treasures and curiosities, which the duke had got together, and the duchess was good-naturedly fond of showing these to her visitors; especially as it gave her an opportunity of talking about her husband—a thing which all good wives like—and hearing other people say how much he was admired and respected; for he was not only a brave man, but an honest and

* The original of this story, which has been, however, considerably enlarged upon, may be found in the history of the Duke of Dantzic, Marshal Lefebvre, one of Napoleon's most respectable, if not most brilliant commanders.

unselfish one, and (what was uncommon in the French generals of those days) more desirous that his companions in arms should receive their share both of praise and pay, than that he should himself be loaded with glory and magnificently rewarded.

The duchess, as we have said, used often to take her friends over the palace, and show them her pictures, vases, richly-wrought armour, beautiful jewels, and other things; but there was one curiosity about which she never said anything, though her dress often brushed past it as the company went on their rounds, and it was so large that you could not help noticing it. This was an enormous wooden chest, twenty feet long—(I can hardly believe this, but so it is said in the history)—long enough, that is, for three full grown men to lie at length inside it, the head of one touching the feet of the next. People were very much puzzled to think what could be in this chest! The duchess did not seem in the least ashamed of it; did not hurry by it; did not give any mysterious sighs as she passed it; but simply behaved as if it did not exist. If anyone said to her, "What a curious old chest that is!" she merely remarked, "Observe, monsieur, the lovely prospect from

this window ; " or, " Madame will doubtless have
noticed that ebony and silver inkstand, and the
writing table to match. It was a little present
to my husband from Marshal Lannes, after the
siege of Dantzic, which of course you've heard
all about." But neither the view from the
window, nor the grand inkstand, nor any of the
other treasures in the room were half so interesting to the duchess's visitors as that old, solid
wooden chest, which seemed to have no history
at all. So of course people set to work to make
one. Some said there was a great hoard of
money bags there—(some even had with their
own eyes, seen the duke taking gold and
silver out of it ;)—others, that there were secret
papers, which would bring him into trouble if
discovered. Some were quite sure it was full of
guns and ammunition, and that one of these
days they would be used in a dreadful con-
spiracy, of which the duke was to be the leader;
some, who had a love for the horrible, maintained that it contained the dead bodies of three
of the duke's friends, which he had had em-
balmed, and for some strange reason or other
refused to have buried. This was the favourite
story, because it was the most shocking and the
most unlikely. Many of the servants in the

house could not be persuaded to go into the
room alone, or after sunset ; in fact, this poor
old chest, standing there in its quiet inoffensive
way, made more noise in the world than if it
had, of its own accord, gone tumbling head over
heels down the grand stone stairs of the palace,
crushing and breaking everything in its course.

At last a lady, who was one of the duchess's
oldest friends, plucked up courage to ask her
what this great secret really was. " Not," she
said, "that you must suppose that I care, or have
the least curiosity on the subject myself. I hope
I'm above nonsense of that kind, and have
something better to think of at my age. But
the world *will* be foolish, you know, my dear
duchess; and for my part, I cannot see the good
of making mysteries. You, and that dear good
duke, whom we all respect from the bottom of
our hearts, are, I am sure, the last persons to
have anything really disgraceful to conceal.
Indeed, I said so myself, only yesterday, when
some one was talking to me on this very subject.
You must not imagine that I ever begin about
it myself; but people, knowing how intimate
I have the honour of being with you, *will*
come and ask me questions. 'Indeed,' I said,
' Madame la Baronne, you may be quite certain

of *that.* I can assure you it is nothing dishonourable either to the duke or the duchess. I have known them for years, and you may rely on what I say. But *what* it is . . . !' however, though I tried hard, I am not sure that I convinced her. People have such bad dispositions."

"Well," the duchess said, trying to smile, but feeling a good deal annoyed, "all I can say is, I am afraid the world will be sadly disappointed when the mystery is unveiled. However, as you truly say, you are one of my oldest friends, and I have not the smallest objection to letting you see what is in this wonderful chest. Perhaps you will not mind stepping this way." She went, followed by her friend, who in truth would have liked to have had a few more difficulties to get over, and already felt that the world was, after all, extremely common-place. "Now," said the duchess, standing before the chest, and unlocking it, "will you help me with this lid? It's rather heavy. Take care of your left hand." The chest was opened, and proved to be full of nothing but old clothes; old silks and velvets, and embroideries, old weather-stained uniforms, old linen; some apparently had been torn up to make bandages—old dresses, some handsome, and even yet scarcely out of fashion, others plainer and simpler. Quite at the bottom of all were some plain, rude garments, such as might have belonged to country people, patched and turned, darned and pieced in a variety of ways, worn and discoloured with hard work. These were what had belonged to the husband and wife in old days, when they were poor, and lived in a humble way in their own little village.

"Ah!" said the duchess, "These are my great treasures. My husband and I often look at them; it is good to remember what we once have been."

This is the end of the story. I should be glad to think, though we are not expressly told so, that some of the treasures stored up in this chest were given away to the poor—having done their work for their first owners. As it is, I am afraid you may think the history rather a disappointing one; but it puts a good example before us, though we are not dukes and duchesses, nor ever likely to be. We have each—have we not, —a great chest, in which we keep our treasures. I mean our memories? Our hearts are like a storehouse, to which every year brings its contribution. If we could open them we should find, as we do in our boxes and drawers, strange things hidden away. Scraps of paper, faded keepsakes, locks of hair; perhaps a torn hand-kerchief, or an old prayer book—(the print surely has got smaller since it was given us)—a dear little pair of tiny socks, a small white frock, (the sleeves will hardly hold three of our fingers,) or, who knows? an old polished walking-stick, that some kind and honoured hand, whose wrinkles were lovely in our eyes, used to lean upon; a half-finished bit of drawing or carpentering that some bright, hopeful boy or girl was called away from before it could be finished; and sadder than all these, some gift from a friend who has deserted us, or for deserting whom we have to reproach ourselves.

Such are some of the treasures in our chests. And in our quiet times, our rainy afternoons, our long summer Sunday evenings, we turn them over and dwell upon them, and perhaps shed a few tears over them. But very few of us are like this good lady. Very few of us, when tempted to be proud of our success, our good prospects, some praise we have received, some advance in the world, however small, are inclined to look back and remember "what we have come from." Very few think of what we were —of what all mankind were—before Christ came

C

to save us; of what we still should be without
Him. Very few men and women like to look
back on their own faults, their own mistakes,
anything that lowers them in their own eyes.
But it was very good advice that a pious and
learned bishop once gave to those who were
tempted to pride—and who is not ?—that they
should every day call to mind one of their
worst sins, or most shameful disgraces, or most
foolish actions; * and when praised or made
much of by others, should turn their thoughts
to something which might remind them of their
own littleness, weakness, and perhaps sinfulness.

At least, let us look back on the past with
thankful hearts, remembering what God has been
pleased to give us, and how many, many bless-
ings we owe to His mercy. And let us, if there
are others poorer or more sorrowful than ourselves, remember our own past trials, and try to
give them the help for which we should in former
days have been so thankful. So we shall be
able to say, from the depths of our heart, " In
all time of our *wealth*," no less than "in all time
of our tribulation," " Good Lord deliver us."

* Jeremy Taylor : Holy Living—" Of Humility."

III.

A CRADLE.

I ONCE told you about a visit to a cottage, and about an old woman and her patchwork counterpane. To-day I am going to describe to you another walk in that same village.

It is a beautiful day in June. As we go along we pick the wild roses from the hedge, some white, some pale clear pink, some with buds of a deeper colour. Once we stand still to listen to the grasshopper, who—what with the sunshine and the delicious air, and the beautiful sights around him—is so happy that he cannot help saying so from his hiding place to every one who passes by. There are the hay-makers hard at work; we can see them through the elm trees. Now we must turn down this lane and follow beside the brook till we get to that single cottage with the old-fashioned windows and moss-grown thatch, with that bush of traveller's joy showing its clusters of white flowers in front.   As we stop and knock at the door we smell the sweet white pinks.   " Come in," says somebody in a low voice, and we go in.   The room looks like Sunday, it is so quiet. There is a wide window-seat with fuchsias and other flowers, through which the sunshine falls in wavering shapes on the grey stone floor, and flickers on an old brown wooden cradle, beside which a beautiful young woman is sitting, with a ragged shirt-sleeve, which she is trying to mend, on her knee, and a book at her side. She looks as if even this little bit of light work were too hard for her; her eyes have the brightness of decline, her hands are wasted, and her voice has that deep sound which one knows too well where there is weakness or disease of the lungs.   " Well, Annie," we said, " and are you staying at home by yourself to mind your little nephew ? "   " Yes," she says, " her brother and sister and all of them are out in the hay-field. Baby is very good and quiet, and gives her no trouble.   Should we like to see him ? "   And we kneel down by the cradle and just peep at the little creature asleep inside it.   Annie tells us how cleverly her brother made the cradle himself out of an old barrel cut in half ;   it certainly was very ingeniously contrived ;   it had done for three or four babies already, beside this one. "Perhaps some day," we say, "one of them may grow up to be a great man, and this cradle will be shown as a curiosity because it was what he had when he was little." Annie laughed and said, "she did not think that very likely; but any how it was a wonderful thing that any of us should have gone into such a small space, and been contented with it once upon a time."

"Aye, and that we should have forgotten all about it too," is our reply.

Annie made no answer, for a bad fit of coughing came on and lasted for some minutes; when it was over she seemed too weak and suffering to speak, and we both sat quite silent, her head leaning back against the cushion of her chair, and her hands lying idle on her knee. The brook tinkled and gurgled outside, and the birds sang in the lane. She looked up presently, without raising her head, and said almost inaudibly in a sad weary tone, "I wonder when *my* cradle will be ready?"

"*Your* cradle, Annie; what do you mean?"

"I daresay the wood that it is to be made of is cut down, and seasoning in some carpenter's yard not far off," she continued.

"You don't mean your coffin?"

"Yes," she said, "a coffin is a sort of cradle." And she glanced at the one in front of her on which the sunbeams were dancing in ever-changing figures.

"My cradle," she said, "won't be covered with an old blanket like that, but with beautiful green grass and daisies. The sun will shine on them, and the birds sing as they are doing now. And Jem and Sally will go out hay-making, and I shan't miss them any more than baby does as he lies there. *Now*, she added with a tearful look, I *do* miss them, and I *do* fret after them, and feel as if I'd give, I don't know how much, for one run round the water meadow, but *then* I shan't. I shan't care for anything, I suppose, then, though now I set my heart on them so."

She stopped for a few moments and then went on. "I know where you picked those roses"—for we had given her the flowers we brought with us—"just before you turn down this lane, close to the old hollow ash tree. Before you brought them I'd been longing and longing for some roses, and now I can hardly bear the sight of them; it seems to make everything harder and harder to leave. Do you know I've never been able to walk as far as that tree since last Michaelmas; I remember it because the haws were just getting red, and the ash leaves falling. It was two months before baby was born." And before we could answer her she went on—" Ah, he'll be finding his legs just as I am losing mine; as he learns to talk, I shall be learning to hold my tongue; by the time he's able to ask for what he wants, I shall have left off wanting anything, or being a trouble to anybody; and so I suppose there'll be an end of me." She spoke a little bitterly, and threw herself back with a deep sigh.

" Annie, you know better than that."

" I'm sure," she answered in a weary tone, " I sometimes wonder what I do know and what I don't. I am certain about *one* thing. I used to think it sounded very pretty and melancholy-like to hear of a girl's dying young, but now it seems as if death were dreadful—dreadful indeed—when he's got hold of you *so*"—and she grasped her left wrist tightly with her poor thin right hand—" and you feel that, struggle as you may, you cannot escape, and that it's only a business of days and weeks, and that you may say good-bye to the roses and the hay-making, and the little house you've been so fond of, and to your own clothes even, and to"—she hesitated and then sobbed out—" everybody that's ever cared for you. Oh, it's a hard, hard, bitter thing ! "

" Nobody can tell how hard," we said, trying to soothe her partly by words, partly by action. However, she soon quieted herself, saying with a mournful smile : " I mayn't even have a good comfortable cry now. The doctor says I mustn't excite myself. Do talk to me a little ; " and she put out her hand affectionately.

" Well Annie, your own words are better than anything we can say. You called your coffin a cradle just now, and I think it was a very good word of yours. Baby has gone to sleep, and has dropped his plaything out of his hand. So you, when you lie down in your coffin, will drop your playthings—for they are but toys after all, most of them—and never miss them in that last sleep.

The baby's frock has no pockets in it. No more will your last garment. " We brought nothing into this world, and it is certain we can carry nothing out." The child, as he lies in the cradle, is quite safe, and peaceful, and happy. Why should not your last rest be the same, if you die in repentance and faith ? As he sleeps there, his father and mother are out at work, earning a living for him, though he knows nothing about it. This is like what it says in the Psalms : He giveth to His beloved in sleep. It is so with us all. Our heavenly Father is making provision for us while we are slumbering, and surely He will not cease to work for our good even when our bodies are laid asleep in the churchyard.

Well then, another thing. As you said at the beginning of our talk, there will come a time when the baby will grow up, and then his cradle will no longer be able to hold him. So there will come a time when we shall rise again from our coffins with glorified bodies, because the grave and death have no more dominion over us. Now, do you suppose that baby could ever understand what he will be able to know and do, and enjoy when he becomes a man ? "

" No," said she, " certainly not."

" Before he went to sleep, all he cared for was breakfast and dinner, and perhaps his rattle, or having a silly little song sung to him, or something like that."

" Yes," she said, " quite true, and I think I see what you mean, only I can't quite explain it."

" I am sure you must.   How can we tell—
we who are but like tired children and must
soon be laid in our cradles, or coffins, whichever
we call it—what it will be to be really grown
up, and how we shall feel when we have got old
enough to leave them altogether ?   Ah, Annie,
you and I are but children !   We can't tell yet
about our real grown-up life in heaven, nor
what pleasure and wisdom, and strength and
greatness there may be in store for us ;   nor
what new powers God may give us for glorify-
ing Him in another world.   You might as well
ask baby to read and explain to you that
chapter in your open Bible there.   You could
not even make him *understand* what you
wanted, much less *do* it.

" I wonder now, Annie, what you care for
most in the world ? "   She blushed up and said
nothing, but her eyes were directed to a
beautiful geranium which stood in the window ;
it had been given her by Tom.   Tom was a
young telegraph clerk who lived in the town
about fifteen miles off, and who always came to
see her once a fortnight, though he knew that
all the bright plans they had had of being married
and setting up a house together had come to
nothing.

"No wonder, Annie, that you care for *that*. It has been the brightest thing in your life, has it not?"

"Yes, and the hardest to leave," she answered, her eyes filling again.

"But if you were to try and make that baby there understand why you and Tom should have so much happiness in loving one another, you would never succeed, would you?" She smiled very sadly.

"Well, now answer me this. When we, who are after all but ignorant children now, have *really* grown up, how can we tell but there may be some love, some happiness for us, compared with which even this feeling you and Tom have for one another is merely a small and insufficient thing?"

"I shouldn't *like* to leave off caring for him," she said, almost angrily.

"No; but I never meant to say another world would do away with any love we had, only give us infinitely more and higher and better love. That child loves its mother, but knows of no other affection; when he is grown up, it is not that he will leave off loving his mother; on the contrary, he will love her more; but his eyes will be open to know of other love of which he dreams not now, and which will make him understand the love of his mother better than he ever did before.   So, in another world, we may feel the love of God in a way we cannot here, and that may throw a new light on all the love we have ever had for our fellow-creatures.   Do you understand now, Annie ? "

She said, in a low voice, that she thought so. Her eyes again went after the geranium : " He brought it me his own self," she said.   " He spends half his wages on me."

" Yes, Annie, but who made the geranium, to begin with ?   And who gave you eyes to see it ? And who put that love for one another into your hearts of which it is a token ? "

" God," she said, with a blush ; " of course I know that."

" And don't you think His love must be as much greater than any other love, as the Maker is greater than the thing made ? "

" I suppose so ; but oh, when Tom comes of a Sunday and sits just here, and talks and brings me things, and perhaps takes hold of my hand, you know it seems like something *real* and *near ;* and the other, ... what you talk of, is so very far off."

" That is just what I meant.   Many things

that are now very real to you would have been very unreal when you were a little child ; so by-and-by things which seem strange now may become realities ; aye, and the realities you will prize beyond all others."

" If I was only good enough ! " said Annie.

" God will help you to be good if you ask Him. . This illness is sent to make you good."

She cast her eyes down for an instant, then colouring deeply, said—" And it isn't wrong, my caring for Tom ? "

" How can it be ? Who knows ? Perhaps this very parting may be the means of your being happier together hereafter than you could have been if you had had all your earthly wishes granted. You must pray for him as well as for yourself."

" Yes," said Annie ; and she said no more, for her mind seemed to be at work, and her face was full of far off thoughts.

After a few minutes we rose and left her. She just said 'a kind word or two of farewell, but her thoughts appeared to be elsewhere ; only her eyes, with a kind of yearning look in them, followed us to the door.

" Come again soon," she said, smiling sweetly.

We never saw her again. She died before the roses had withered; and was laid, as she had said, under the turf of the village churchyard.

Tom used to come there every other Sunday. He used to steal up to her grave in the twilight, and perhaps an hour later you might pass him coming down the churchyard path, but it would be too dark to see if there were any tears on his face. It is years ago since then, and he went on steadily working in his old place. Hardly any one knew, few would have guessed, his story.

He died about six months since, in one of those sad railway accidents. People wondered he had never married on his high wages, though when he died they said it was a good thing he did not leave a widow and children. But the clergyman of his parish says they will never get another to set the example he did, and be such a friend and adviser to the lads and younger men employed at the station. A word from him went further than a sentence from another. The baby, Annie's little nephew, is a fine high-spirited school-boy. The only thing that remains just as it was is the old cradle. And sometimes when I go to the cottage I think of Annie's beautiful wistful face. that summer afternoon, and wonder if she could come back to life here what answer she would be able to give to the questions we talked of that day, but a very little while before she died ; and what Tom and she think of it all now.

IV.

BY THE FIRE SIDE.

I HAVE often wished to say a little about Fire, but have been kept back, because it was such a great and terrible thing. Fire seemed, the more one thought of it, the strangest mixture of good and evil that the world presents. To-day, I can only suggest a very few thoughts in a very few words to you, leaving much unsaid.

What may be called the *bad* and dreadful aspect of Fire, really brings such awful thoughts before us, that when they came to be written down, they seemed too solemn for a book of this kind. And perhaps they will come into most minds without being talked about or discussed. About the good and kindly qualities of fire, however, we may attempt to speak—and it is a subject that is sure to come home to one and all of us.

But what *is* fire? Who can tell us? Let us look it out in the dictionary. We find "fire" explained as "the igneous element," or "anything burning."

I hope, my dear friends, you are much the wiser—but putting an English word of four letters into two long Latin ones, seems a round-about way of explaining it. And a person who did not know that fire was in the habit of burning till he saw the fact in a book, must have begun his education at the wrong end.

Well, then, what *is* fire? We do not know, except that it is something very pure, very bright, very swift, very hot, very unsubstantial, very full of life. Something that you cannot touch, something that you cannot hold, something that makes your eyes and your heart glad to look at, something that is born in a moment, but never rests till it has destroyed those very things that its life depended on.

We do not know anything, except perhaps nursing some one in a bad illness, that takes such complete possession of one's thoughts as lighting a fire, and coaxing it to burn. How often we all have done so, kneeling before it, striking a match, seeing how the little blue flame spreads to the paper or straw—aye, it is catching the twigs now. Now it flares up, then dies down, leaving the wood-ashes a glowing red fast turning to grey!

D

Will it catch that little bit of cinder? It tries, but there is not enough air. We must take a few of those heavy lumps of coal away, and try again. Ah! that is better. Now we have given it a chance. Do you hear the fizzing of the gas? That means it has really caught. Now another tiny bit of coal, just among these blazing sticks. Ah, the merry crackling sound! And the blaze begins to dart about the room, and the smoke to mount the chimney. I think our fire will *do* now, don't you?

It has often been said that lighting a fire is the first thing a man does when he means to live in any place, even for a night. If we see a heap of cinders on a common, or on the skirts of a wood, we probably guess there has been a gipsy encampment there. We talk about our hearth, our fire side, when we mean our home, that which makes the life and comfort of our home.

So we know fire was considered a very sacred thing, standing as it did for a type, first of the well-being of a family, then of that of a city. At Rome there was a sacred fire which was never allowed to go out, and a certain number of holy women, who were called vestal virgins, were always employed in watching it. They were expected to be women of the highest character

and great respect was paid to them. It would
be well if in Christian countries people took as
much trouble to keep up the fire of love to God
and devotion towards Him, as these heathen did
to preserve the fire on the altar of their goddess
Vesta. And this leads us to say a few words on
the spiritual meaning of fire.

First of all, its *purity*. Fire, as we all are
aware, has a most wonderful power of cleansing.
After any one has had an infectious complaint,
we know how valuable it is in this respect. It
has often been said, that the famous fire of
London, in 1666, was, in one way, the greatest
possible blessing, because it carried away all
traces of the dreadful plague which had visited
the city the year before. And we know what an
effect fire has in purifying the air, say of a sick-
room. So, in a spiritual sense, may the heavenly
fire purge our corrupt hearts and minds. When
Isaiah had that wonderful vision in the temple,
before he was called to go and take his message
to the house of Israel, he said, " Woe is me,
for I am a man of unclean lips." And we are
told that one of the seraphim* flew towards him

---

* The name "seraph," is very probably taken from a word
meaning *to burn*. So Milton says :—
"Let the bright seraphim in burning row,
Their loud uplifted angel trumpets blow."

with a live coal, which he had taken with the tongs from off the altar, and laid it on his mouth, saying, "Lo! this hath touched thy lips, and thine iniquity is taken away, and thy sin purged." What a grand and most expressive figure of the gift of the Holy Spirit to all those who are to carry God's message upon their lips to mankind! How pure such lips ought to be from everything low, vile, and unclean.   Nor was it only *purity* that was meant.   The prophet's lips were to burn with the *fervour* of inspired eloquence. "Thoughts that breathe and words that burn" were to be his.   Any of you who have ever heard a great speaker, know what this means. As he stands up among the crowd, his eye kindling with eagerness, his features beaming with life, his hands, his body, the very crest of hair that tosses above his brow, the quick-following words that burst irresistibly forth from his glowing and passionate heart, all seem to have something fiery about them, and if one looks round at the countenances of the listeners, they too are kindling with that spiritual fire.   First it catches one, then another.   Dull faces light up, young and ardent faces seem to burn with strong excitement and emotion.   Here and there are a few damp sticks that nothing will inflame.   But they are soon lost in the great conflagration, as we may call it—the blaze and glow of eager feeling that starts up on all sides. Hark to the shouts, the cheering, the overwhelming applause! The speaker has kindled a fire in a thousand hearts. That one man is like the small flame or tiny spark that sets fire to a whole city. For good or for evil, "life and death are in the power of the tongue."

But does the fire stand for anything else? Aye, truly; for the warm glow of *love*, for the power of cheering and comforting the sorrowful, the starved, and the homeless. You know what it is to feel at times as if a fire were everything to you. In former days, people used to talk about "cold grief," and it seems very true to nature to say so. The real bodily feeling of cold, that comes on with sorrow of heart, is one of the most dreary some of us have ever experienced.

In a house where there has been a death, have you never noticed how cold—literally cold—the mourners are who were most nearest of kin to the dead? Bodily weakness, want of food and fresh air, exhaustion—all these things seem to take away from the warmth and glow of life. Such persons as these one may see creeping up to the fire, seeking its warm and kindly smile, and finding there a comfort which touches first the body and then the mind. Oh, if we could comfort like that! could warm with our love some poor, cold, starved miserable hearts! What a generous thing a fire is. It does not grudge its warmth. It glows for the king and the beggar alike. It is like some one whose love embraces the world; whose large heart takes in high and low—aye, the very dogs and cats that come and bask in its warmth; or, as we sometimes see in a farm-house kitchen, the unfledged bird, who is brought to be cherished before it; or the little brown crickets whom it makes so glad.

Now and then we see men and women, warm, generous, unselfish, people, who have some of that spirit of love. Do we not know the grasp of their hand and the glance of their eye? Do we not tell them, or rather, do they not guess, our troubles? Does not a hearty, cheerful word or two from them clear away misgivings, doubts, suspicions, regrets, that we may have cherished for weeks? Do not the very children, the very animals, love them? Do not the very insects feel something of their tenderness and genial kindness? Why should we not copy them?

But is there no other quality which the fire
possesses? Yes, surely—*Light.* The sun itself,
which lights the world, is but one gigantic fire.
So light is one of the gifts of God's Holy Spirit.
The hymn, called *Veni Creator,* (used at ordina-
tions of the clergy), begins—

> "Come, Holy Ghost, our souls inspire,
> And *lighten* with *celestial fire;*
> Thou the Anointing Spirit art,
> That dost thy seven-fold gifts impart ;
> Thy blessed unction from above
> Is comfort, life, and fire of love ;
> Enable with perpetual *light*
> The dulness of our blinded sight.

And so in the Book of Revelation we are
told, "There were seven lamps of fire burning
before the throne, which are the seven spirits of
God."

So, in the collect for Whit-Sunday, we say,
" God, who as at this time didst teach the hearts
of thy faithful people, by sending to them the
light of thy Holy Spirit. Grant us by the same
Spirit to have a right judgment in all things, and
evermore to rejoice in His holy comfort." So,
those who were baptized, were spoken of as
having been *enlightened :* Heb. vi, 4.

It would be impossible to say here a tenth
part of what might be said about Light; and

again, about spiritual light, giving us a clear insight into the meaning of God's word, or a right judgment as to what our own course of life ought to be ; or a right understanding of His dealings with us ; or a knowledge of our own hearts ; or of the hearts of those with whom we have to do. But this also was no doubt typified, like all the other gifts and graces of the Holy Spirit, by those tongues of fire that came down on the day of Pentecost, and sat upon the heads of the Apostles—

> " When the faithful were assembled
>   On the day of Pentecost ;
> Rushed the wind, the place it trembled,
>   Came from heaven the Holy Ghost ;
> Golden shower of consecration,
>   Tongues of fire were on them shed,
> And that holy dedication
>   Made an altar of each head." *

This brings us to the last point we shall touch

* Hymn for Whit-Sunday, in the Bishop of Lincoln's *Holy Year.* The hymn quoted above would be found a most instructive one for the present purpose. May we be permitted here to testify from experience to the extreme value of the " Holy Year" for learning by heart in Sunday-schools. Almost every hymn in it may be made the basis of explanatory reading, in connection with the Sundays and Festivals ; and no adequate idea of its theological teaching, as a whole, can be formed from the selections from it, now become so common.

upon—the fire of *devotion*. Perhaps there is no image in the world that so forcibly gives the idea of the consecration and devotion of a man's life— his very self, to the service of God, as this of an Altar. Placed, it may be, on a high hill, the world at its feet, with nothing between it and the sky, its whole heart on fire ; all the low material substances of earth consumed, devoured, sacrificed, to this one great, all-engrossing end of the glory of God. There is nothing impure, nothing cold, nothing dull. All is kindled into a lively flame that stretches its long arms up- ward, still upward, disdaining the earth, and seeking only those things which are above. Far and wide the glory of that noble burnt-offering spreads and streams abroad. It lights up and warms this world ; but all its aspirations, all its longings, are for another. It is not like a bon- fire, kindled for the honour of man, in compli- ment to some prince, or noble, or victorious general. It is something far sublimer, far purer, far grander, and better than that. It is giving our best to the Lord our Maker. Men may admire the sacrifice, or they may scorn it, and say, " Wherefore this waste ? " But it was not offered to win the praise of man, but the acceptance of God. So if God ever gives us an

opportunity of sacrificing anything to Him, be
it our money, our talents, our time, our health,
our affections, or what is often hardest of all,
our own will, may we feel and speak, " Who
am I, and what is my people, that we should be
able to offer so willingly after this sort ?   All
things come of thee, O Lord, and of thine own
own have we given thee." So may fire from
heaven descend, as it did on the sacrifices of
Abraham,* of Elijah, and of Solomon, and God
accept us and ours for Jesus Christ's sake, our
great Sacrifice, and our Everlasting High Priest.
May He cleanse our hearts with the fire of
holiness; may He quicken them with zeal ;
may He warm them with love; may He
enlighten their darkness and ignorance ;   and
above all, may He kindle in them a glowing and
ardent devotion to Himself, that shall burn away
all our worldliness, our littleness, our meanness,
and selfishness, and daily bring us nearer and
nearer to His heavenly dwelling place.

* Gen. xv, 17 ; 1 Kings xviii ; 2 Chron. vii.

V.

PHOTOGRAPHS.

———

TWENTY-FIVE years ago, if any boy or girl in one of our National schools had met with this dreadfully hard word in a book, they would most likely have made as many difficulties over it as some horses do when they are wanted to leap a stiff fence or six-barred gate. It really is not fair to call upon any one to spell such a word. And as to telling us the meaning of it . . . . ! that would be *quite* too much to expect.

Well, and now, in 1874, one can hardly pass a day without this hard word forcing himself, somehow or other, upon us. Our books, our newspapers, our sitting rooms, our shops, aye, even our pockets are all over-run with photographs. Photography is like that water-weed which only came into the country a few years ago, and spread so fast as nearly to choke up some of our rivers. Go where you will, you meet with photographs—and yet more photographs.

One finds oneself in an out of the way little village, with a bit of common where only the geese and donkeys and school-boys used to enjoy themselves, and, lo! and behold, there is a photographer's shop on wheels. One stops at a tiny little way-side inn, which looks as old fashioned as Lord Nelson himself, in his blue coat and cocked hat, painted upon the sign, and there, on the parlour table, is the carte-de-visite book with the portraits of all the family—of the master of the house in his Sunday waistcoat, and a very large pair of boots; of the mistress sitting, for a wonder, with her hands before her, and looking as if she disliked being so idle, and was sure the girl in the kitchen would let the meat be burnt to a chip now her back was turned; of the eldest girl with her hair done up in great stuffy plaits on the top of her head, and looking as if somebody had just set her off laughing at the wrong moment; of the eldest boy, with a gilt watch-chain, and a very large gold ring—he is in business in London, but in the photograph he is leaning on one of the pillars of a ruined temple, and has a large waterfall tumbling and tossing behind him.

Then there are Totty, and Billy, and Joe,

the three youngest children, all in a group. Totty and Billy are pretty good, only the checks on their plaid frocks, somehow, look too big and staring. Joe was very miserable cutting a double tooth, and had got his finger in his mouth up to the last minute. Totty had snatched hold of his hand to prevent his being taken in that attitude, and that is why he looks so cross. And here is dear old granny in her arm-chair, almost the only one who looks natural. There she sits, as still as she always did, with her Bible and her bit of knitting, and her little old black shawl. It is nice to have that to remember her by now she is gone.

So again, if we go into a court of justice. There is a trial going on ; perhaps it is the Tichborne case, in which you know so much was said of the photograph of the real Sir Roger, and whether his ears were like those of the Claimant. Perhaps it is a breach of promise case. The plaintiff has carried about the defendant's photograph in her pocket these three years. There it is, with a very touching inscription at the back. See what an effect that photograph, so carefully treasured, with its worn well-used edges, has upon the jury. How they put their heads together over it ! We feel quite sure ourselves, that they will find for the plaintiff, as of course they ought. Or some criminal has escaped justice, and has run away, and is in hiding somewhere or other. Unluckily for him the detectives have got hold of his "carte-de-visite," and are circulating copies of it among themselves. There is no mistaking that bushy eyebrow—that projecting under-jaw will betray him, disguise himself as he may. There is an awkward scar there on the left temple; I wonder how he came by it? It will be strange if he is not identified by its means.

We leave the court of justice, or the police station, and go out into the streets. Photographs again! Here is a shop full of them, with a little crowd at the window. There you can see the whole of the Royal Family, and find out what sort of shirt-collars the princes wear, and how the princesses have their hair arranged and their dresses made. As to knowing what they themselves are *like* from their carte-de-visites, that is another thing. Should any of us like to be judged of by our photographs? Oh, surely not! Then there are all the great and clever men, who make the speeches in Parliament; what very wrinkled, careworn faces they have. Then there are some of the great preachers, or good, devoted clergymen. Almost all look tired, thin, anxious, and over-worked. Here are the men who have written clever books on various subjects. How much older they all are than we fancied! Here are the great actresses, singers, and dancers at the theatre. Many of them are surprisingly stout and middle-aged, and look very little like princesses dying for love, or fairy-queens, or sylphs that float in a light and airy way among dewdrops and moonbeams ; and yet we know to-morrow night they will infallibly act those very parts, and be much applauded in them. Certainly, seeing celebrated public characters in a photograph shop is rather disappointing on the whole. Let us try how it will be in private life.

You, perhaps, went this morning to be photographed. You looked in the glass before you went, and were pretty well satisfied with the sit of your collar, and tolerably well pleased with your own face, though there were one or two little wrinkles you could have wished away. You came back, about two hours later than you intended, a good deal the worse for the sickly smell of the chemicals, very tired, very hungry, and with the conviction that your photograph would come out what you yourself were—very cross through having tried to force up an unnatural smile when the man told you to look rather more good-natured—if you could! Oh, what an insulting " if." If you had a child with you, it probably· set up a howl when the man bobbed his head under that funereal-looking black velvet thing that covers the box, and was about five minutes before it could be quieted, thereby spoiling the expression of its own face, and much disturbing yours. After a day or two, the photographs come home. Your husband, the moment he sees yours, bursts out laughing, instead of, as you had hoped, pressing it to his heart, and calling it a " beloved image," or some pretty poetical thing of that kind. One of them more horrid than the rest, some kind friend carries round, and asks everybody if they haven't often seen you look like that ? All the other people giggle in a way that is enough to aggravate patient Grizel herself, who perhaps would not have been so patient if she had lived in the days of cartes-de-visite. As to the child's face, it is a mere blur in one picture and a ferocious grin in another. You take what you think the least ugly of the photographs to your own very particular friend, and she perhaps, with an odd little twitch of the corners of her mouth, tries to say gravely, that it certainly hasn't done you justice. The tip of your nose is too thick, and your mouth does not always look so like the slit in a poor-box, as it does there. But even she seems to be more amused by it than you quite like.

Now why is it that photographs are such disappointing things?

For three or four very good reasons. First of all, because we often have much too good an opinion of ourselves to begin with, and do not like being let down in our own estimation. Secondly, because nearly everybody is a little affected and self conscious when they are being taken, and that is sure to spoil everything.

But there are many people who are neither vain nor affected, whose photographs are a great disappointment to their friends. Some of the faces we care for most *never* come out well in a photograph. You might as well try to give some one who had never seen the sea a notion of what it was like, by bringing home a bucket of salt water. The *material* is there, but the *life* is gone. This is particularly true with middle-aged, worn, anxious, or suffering faces, (and how many of the countenances we love belong to this list!)

E

Photographs give the wear and tear of the body, but they cannot give the immortal loveliness of the soul. Sometimes one gets a photograph of a dear old friend, done—say, in their last illness. All the former health and beauty has faded, the face is thin and drawn, the head droops, the eyes are colourless and weak, the whole look is full of distress, and pain, and languor. Who could call *that* a likeness? Who could call *any*thing a likeness that merely gave the tired lines and hollows of care and fatigue ; or again, the worried look of anxiety, or the hard cold look of business, or the stiff artificial smile assumed for appearance sake? Oh that some one could paint for us our friends as they look when they are really themselves at their best times. When they are saying or doing something kind, when they rise from their prayers, or from reading their Bibles, when they are looking at something beautiful, or listening to something grand and noble. What photographer's art can give us *that?* So in public life. The great speaker is not *himself* when he is sitting in the photographer's chair, but when he is all alive, and as it were possessed, with the grandeur of his own eloquence; the other great people in the same way are not *themselves*, but when something comes to bring out the soul within them. The parts of them that the photograph preserves are their mere outside, the shell and husk of their real selves. And if anybody calls this being "true to nature," we must say that they ought instantly to apologise to both nature and truth for such an affront.

Sometimes on a tombstone we see, "Here rests all that is mortal of So-and-so." If it were not playing with too serious a subject, we might well transfer the inscription to a photograph book. " Here rests all that is mortal of our friends." Their coats and hats, their bonnets and dresses. (How old-fashioned they look already.) Their tired faces, their wrinkles, their ugliness, their awkward figures, their ungraceful stature, their ill health, the Bath chairs they have to sit in, the crutches they have to lean on, the trumpets they have to hold to their ears, the spectacles they could not do without, their false hair, their artificial eyes or teeth—in fact everything that betokens human weakness, human incompleteness, human care, and human trouble.

Oh that some angel's hand could paint for us their real portraits, that spiritual body, which, as we trust, they will wear beyond the grave, that beauty which is not of earth, that loveliness of soul which now and then flashes through the poorest and least attractive of mortal faces, but which can only shine forth in its fulness in a purer and happier world !

> " O how glorious and resplendent
>   Fragile body shalt thou be,
> When endued with so much beauty,
>   Full of health, and strong, and free ;
> Full of vigour, full of pleasure,
>   That shall last eternally ! "

VI.

THIEVES.

WE have one great treat sometimes, when we have earned a holiday by working harder than usual, and that is, to walk across the park and see our kind neighbour, Lady Cecil Harding. It is always pleasant to go where you are sure of a hearty welcome, and at this time of year the walk is an enjoyment in itself. The beech trees in the avenue are coming out, and the young leaves, with their pale downy green just bursting from their pink and golden cases, make one stand still over and over again to wonder at them. Talk of flowers! They are not to be compared to these lovely young beech leaves, and I wonder all the poets in the world do not write verses about them.

Somehow the Hall does not seem quite so cheerful as usual this morning. The drawing-room blinds are still down, and there does not appear to be any life about the place. However the man who opens the door says her ladyship is at home. He looks very grave.

" Is there anything the matter ? "

" Haven't we heard that the house was broken into last night, and all the plate and jewels stolen ?"

"No indeed."

The poor man looks so unhappy and distressed about it, that we feel almost as sorry for him as for the owner of the property, and he goes on to tell us how they've telegraphed from both the railway stations, and to London, and Liverpool, but as yet nothing has been heard of the thieves, and no one in the house saw them, or can describe what they looked like.

The pretty little morning room has evidently not been entered by the thieves ; everything is as usual ; the writing table with the morning's letters, the book Lady Cecil and her daughter were reading, the conservatory beyond, with its heaths and camellias. Miss Harding comes in from the garden—she is Lady Cecil's only unmarried daughter, and very clever, bright, and pretty. As she stands there, with her fresh smiling face, in her plain grey dress, with two or three primroses fastened in front, we cannot help thinking she looks just as well, and just as complete a lady, as if she were covered with jewels, and clad in satin and lace.

" Well, you've heard our news ? " she says.

" Yes, I cannot say how sorry I am."

" I suppose I ought to be sorry too," she replied ; "but I can't bring myself to be as miserable as I ought ; I have just been telling Plummer, who is most broken-hearted of all, that he will have quite a holiday now those old silver dish-covers and soup-ladles are gone, that he had to be for ever rubbing up ; but he doesn't seem altogether comforted. The coolest thing was that the thieves used our own chintz chair-covers and sofa pillow-cases as bags to carry off our property in; the drawing room has been quite stripped."

We were half amused and half shocked as she expected us to be.

" Well, you know, when Mrs. Muffin came to me with a long face this morning, and said ' I've some very bad news for you, miss,' all I thought was of mamma having another of her attacks, so I felt quite a weight off my mind when I learnt it was only the family plate.—Here she is."

Lady Cecil Harding came in and shook hands with us in her kind way. She was over sixty, a widow, and rather quiet always; and to-day she seemed a good deal upset.

"It has made me quite nervous," she said. "At my time of life it seems foolish to care for such things, and I suppose my caring so much just proves how necessary it was that I should learn to do without them. I *had* got fond of some of the old treasures. There was a gold snuff-box your father (turning to Miss Harding) had given him in Paris by the Emperor of Russia."

"Oh yes, and that beautiful bracelet of yours; and the four great silver candlesticks—oh dear, so there were; and all kinds of small trinkets, and the great pieces of plate for the centre of the table; more things than I can count."

"One thing I *am* glad of," said Lady Cecil Harding, "that we let Eleanor have those diamonds for the Queen's drawing room."

"Yes, wasn't it good of my mother?" said Miss Harding, to me. "You know our diamonds have been in the family for years and years, and are the pride of all our hearts; in fact, they have quite a history belonging to them. They were left by the Duchess of Marlborough (Queen Anne's Duchess) to her god-daughter, Lady Sarah Molyneux, who married a Harding, and they have been treasured by us ever since. I persuaded mamma, very much against her will, to let my sister-in-law have them for the last drawing room ; and you see it was most fortunate, for' they are the only things we have saved."

" It is curious;" said Lady Cecil Harding, " one very seldom regrets having done a kind thing ; but it was all your doing my dear;" and she patted her daughter's hand. " Another thing she persuaded me to do, that I am so glad now I did. When my dear husband was High Sheriff, his tenants, who were very fond of him, all subscribed to present him with a splendid silver cup. I shall never forget how pleased he was with this. It was really a beautiful thing, so much more solid and simple than those things generally are. One of the last things he was interested in before he died was the rebuilding of a little church, in a very poor part of his property, and once or twice he said half seriously, 'That cup of mine would just do for a chalice for Hurst church ;' but he never exactly asked to have it given. Afterwards, however, Lucy here persuaded me to ask the clergyman if it might be used as part of the communion plate, and I am so glad now, for it would have broken my heart if the thieves had had it, instead of its being saved for such a purpose as that."

Here a servant came in with a telegram to say the police would be over in a short time to take an exact survey of the spot, and thinking we might be in the way, we took our leave. Lady Cecil saying with a smile, when her daughter was out of hearing, "Don't think too hardly of an old woman for 'loving that well which she must leave ere long.' It's a good lesson for me, and one I wanted more than I supposed."

We walked slowly home under the beech trees, following out the thoughts she had begun. Yes, we were all living in houses that might at any time be broken into. Death is a thief whom no policemen can keep off. No yard-dogs, no watchmen's rattles, no sentries at the door, no Bramah locks, nor patent window-shutters, can keep this robber out. He enters our house silently, irresistibly, perhaps suddenly, and when

we least expect him. Yesterday we were rich,
to-morrow we shall have nothing—Nothing?
That depends. Some of us may, like my kind-
hearted old friend, have bestowed their best
treasures for the good of others. These are
indeed only lent ; they will be restored to them
again hereafter—more precious than before.

Or, better still, they may have devoted them
to the service of God—out of the reach of
death—where no thief approacheth, neither moth
corrupteth. That silver can never become dim,
that fine gold can never undergo change. Have
we any treasures, any of us here? Not diamonds,
not rubies, not plate, but treasures equally dear,
things that no money could buy. Our sight and
hearing, our strength, our time, our powers,
perhaps, in some cases, our money too.

Have we locked them all up, as it were, in
the iron chest of our hard selfish hearts, or are
we lending them, and giving them, and spending them for God's sake, for man's sake, and for
the sake of our own souls? Mind, we cannot
keep the thief out, we can only be beforehand
with him. This very night our souls may be
required of us, and then whose shall these
things be? Turn the double lock, push back

the heavy door, lighten the loaded shelves, enrich the world, and believe me you will be none the poorer yourselves.   Remember the old saying—

"There was a man, though some did count him mad,
The more he cast away, the more he had."

VII.

CLEAN HANDS.

WHAT is there more delightful in the world than the sense of purity and cleanliness, of washing off the stains and soils of life, and leaving behind all the defilements of our old past labour and sorrow? One must be a Londoner, however, or live in some other large and smoky town, quite to know the full comfort of washing one's hands. I say "hands" more especially, because they are the parts of our body which usually have most to do with other people and things. If our hands are not clean we soil everything we touch, and, so to speak, make the whole world our enemy. So, the having clean hands, implies fitness for any work one may be called upon to do. The water has carried away all that had soiled and polluted them, and now they come out in the beautiful pink and white which, nature intended them to wear, shining, and fresh, and pure. They may handle the folds of snowy satin without injuring it ; they may be placed beside a lily in all her whiteness and not be put to shame. It is natural, therefore, that to say any one has "clean hands," should be a figurative way of saying he is true and just and faultless in all his dealings, and fit to be trusted with any undertaking.

We know how it was when we were children. Before our mothers would allow us to take hold of anything they valued, they would say, "Let me look at your hands. Both of them. Front and back. Are your fingers *quite* clean? Very well, then, if you are careful, I will lend you this book, or this toy," or whatever the desired object might be.

Now, it is just the same when we are grown up. People are always wishing to know if those whom they employ have "clean hands." Beginning with the rulers of the country. We hear it sometimes asked, Have *they* clean hands ? or have they soiled them by seeking their own interest, instead of that of the nation, whose business they administer? Members of Parliament—have *they* clean hands, or have they climbed into their places by any mean and degrading ways? Voters — have *they* clean hands, or have they been dirtied by bribery and corruption ? Men who hold any office in Church and State—have *they* clean hands, or have they been stained by baseness, dishonesty, flattery of great people, dishonourable behaviour of whatever kind ? Farmers and tradesmen — have *they* clean hands ? Free from the pollutions of the shop or the market ; from unfair gains and underhand transactions ; from passing off unsound wares for sound ones; from short measures and light weights ; from puffing and dishonest advertising and trickery ; from hardness to the poor, and servility to the rich ; from harshness and injustice to those in their pay ; from taking unkind advantage of the misfortunes of those in their own special line of business ? Working men and women—have *they* clean hands, or is there clinging to them any mark of fraud or falsehood ; any wages unfairly earned, any pay received for services which they would be ashamed to own ; anything stolen, anything kept back or hidden ; any price paid for sin ; any money entrusted to them for the use of others, which they have turned aside to their own profit ; any skimpy, faulty, bad work, looking sound on the surface, but rotten underneath ? Let us all take heed to ourselves. Clean hands and a pure heart are what God will require of us, and without these we can never hope to present ourselves before Him and live.

But there is another stain upon the hands of some, and that is the stain of blood. It was thus that the hand of Cain was stained when he slew his brother Abel. And oh, how many since, in all ages, have had that deadly and fatal curse clinging to their hands. Alas! that we should have to speak so plainly of a sin which the mind recoils from, but which makes itself seen and heard of every day in our midst. Oh, you fathers and mothers, when you indulge your hasty tempers, when you stimulate your passions by strong drink and high words, think what a training you are giving to your children, even if you care nothing for your own souls. Cain was an innocent child once, lying on the bosom of Eve. All the murderers, of whose crime the newspapers are full, were once boys and girls, harmless and happy as your own. How many a man, spending his last night on earth, in the condemned cell of one of our great closely-watched prisons—or walking, with all eyes upon him, to the very foot of the gallows—can trace the beginning of sin to the indulgence of some hasty temper in childhood, inherited perhaps from a father or mother who took no pains to conquer their own.

Some one here may this very day have yielded to bad temper, have kicked or struck a child or a companion ; have flown out in hasty oaths and bad language ; or have given way to brooding gloom and sulkiness. They must not take it amiss if we remind them that they have, by so doing, put one foot on the murderer's ladder, a ladder that goes down and down, step by step, to the pit of hell itself. No human power, we know, can do away with the stain of blood-guiltiness. Our greatest English poet felt this so strongly that he described in words which some of us may know already, a wretched lady, who, with her husband, had murdered King Duncan, their guest, in hopes of succeeding to his kingdom. No one but themselves knew of the murder. They were great and powerful. So far all had succeeded with them. But no great-ness, no success, could give back the quiet untroubled sleep of innocence. The miserable woman is brought before us walking restlessly in her sleep, clothed in her night-dress, carrying a candle, and then feverishly trying to wash her hands from the stains of blood, which in her fancy still clung to them—" Out, damned spot !

F

out, I say! What, will these hands ne'er be clean? Here's the smell of the blood still. All the perfumes of Arabia will not sweeten this little hand. Oh, oh, oh!" Ah, it is all in vain. Waking or sleeping, the stain of blood will evermore be there.

Solemn and terrible as this description is, I have often thought it must have been suggested by one still more awful. You know what I mean, When Pilate, seeing that he could prevail nothing, but that rather a tumult was made, took water and *washed his hands* before the multitude, saying, "I am innocent of the blood of this just person. See ye to it."

I do not know whether you will think so too, but I have always felt that—in contrast to the nobleness expressed by "having clean hands" —there was something unworthy and unfeeling in such language as "I wash my hands of him ; I wash my hands of the business." It is like Cain saying, "Am I my brother's keeper?" There are two things we *cannot* wash our hands of— responsibility beforehand, and guilt afterwards. We cannot wash our hands of our fathers, mothers, brothers, husbands, wives, children, or neighbours. We may *say* we do so, but we cannot, any more than Pilate, by washing his hands was freed from blame before God. We are born with duties to some people. We cannot get rid of their claim upon us, however inconvenient we may find it to fulfil that claim. And some day those unfulfilled duties will rise up before us, like the ineffaceable stains of which we have already spoken, and cry out against us as the voice of Abel's blood cried from the ground, and witnessed against Cain in the ear of the Almighty Judge of all.

We ought not to desire to wash our hands of *responsibility*. We all ought to desire to be cleansed from stains of *guilt*. Who can do this for us ? We can all answer that question. We know who it was who, on the night of His betrayal, took a towel and girded himself, and began to wash the feet of his disciples. We know what St. Peter then said to him, "Lord, not my feet only, but also my *hands* and my head." Pilate might take water and wash his hands before the multitude, but never be able to cleanse them. But there is no guilt, however deep, that Christ cannot and will not wash away. Let any of us think of this ; any who have been walking on life's way and doing life's work with sin-defiled hands. The stain of dishonour may be there, the stain of corruption may be there, the stain of earthliness may be there, the deadly stain of blood itself may be there. The beautiful, the noble, the pure, may meet you in their shining garments, and may offer you their white and blameless hands. You draw back. It is not for the like of you to touch them. Every one of your fingers would leave its mark behind. You shrink away from the strangers and try to keep on the other side of the road.

But what if, in the midst of that hot dusty way, you should see a tall, steadfast rock throwing its shadow over the path? Green moss, beautiful feathery ferns, luxuriant grasses, show there must be water near, Water, bursting from the very heart of the rock, where some natural shock, be it tempest or earthquake, has made a breach in the stony barrier. Do you not hasten to the spring, and bathe your stained, dusty, heated hands beneath it? The sun strikes on the water, and a thousand rainbows are dancing among the crystal drops. Where are the stains, where is the shame, where is the misery and disgrace? The water flowing from that smitten Rock has taken them all away. Need this parable be interpreted? Is it not familiar to every child among us? We know what Rock has been smitten for us. "That Rock," says St.

Paul, "was Christ." When He was hanging on the cross, the spear of the soldier pierced His side, and forthwith came thereout blood and water. That fountain, believe me, has never ceased to flow. No winter's cold can freeze and harden it, no summer's sun can dry it up. It is not a spring shut up, a fountain sealed, a well kept under lock and key, for the benefit of a few. It is a wayside spring, whither every traveller may come. All may drink of it. All may wash in it. Our defilements have no power to pollute it. It is not like a river running through a town, black and noisome with the dirt and misery of the dark streets and poor smoky houses. It makes us clean, but we cannot make it unclean. Clear and bright, full of life, full of health, on and on it flows. O, come hither, and wash away your sin! Be not ashamed to own your sin. The very waters which reflect those stains and impurities are ready to carry them away where they will never be brought up against you more. "Wash me throughly from my wickedness, and cleanse me from my sin. For I acknowledge my faults, and my sin is ever before me." And then all our work will be holy. Whatever we put our hands to will have God's blessing upon it. We shall be able to say with

Moses, whose rod brought the water for God's people from the stricken Rock in the wilderness, " Prosper thou the work of our hands upon us. O prosper thou our handy work."

VIII.

A NEEDLE AND THREAD.

WHAT is going to be said in this paper is entirely . for women. (Therefore we may be tolerably sure that any man who takes up this book will pick it out to read. For it is so nice to listen to good advice meant for some one else.) But the fact is, I want to say a little about some tiny . clever friends and companions we have who live in our work-boxes, and who are perhaps the most faithful and constant helpers many of us possess. We are so fond of them that we keep them wrapped up in new flannel. One or other of them is almost always in our hands—indeed we have known some women so strongly attached to them, that they might generally be seen with two or three stuck into the front of their gowns, and certainly very near their hearts.

No wonder! They are so bright, and quick, and industrious, and have such a cheerful way of clicking over their work as if they liked it.

The stiffer it is the more they click and the merrier they seem. It is quite beautiful to see how fast they will go when in good hands, like a flash of lightning, or a railway engine; and just as the engines have a long train of carriages after them, so our brisk little friends have a long thread, often twenty or thirty times as long as themselves, which they drag up and down, and in and out, through hems and seams, raw edges and selvages, silk and cotton, calico and flannel, new clothes and old, corduroy and cloth, with all the life and spirit imaginable. They dash at their work as eagerly as a cat does after a mouse, or they glide through it as softly as the same cat does when she is picking her way among crockery ware.

They can go at any pace. Little stitches, big stitches, long stitches, short stitches, loose stitches, tight stitches, stitches in time, stitches after time. Only tell them what they are to do, and they will do it, or snap in the attempt.

Don't we see people like that sometimes? People who keep everything going, and are, as we say, "the life and soul" of any party where they may be. Such persons are always starting fresh plans and ideas, and everybody else comes to them and says, "Can't *you* think of something?"—because it is to them that their neighbours look in a difficulty. If there are any mothers of families here, they have most likely one such child, who is to the others what the needle is to the thread. The sharp one, the quick one, the ready one, the maker of plans, the one who takes the lead, and whose words all the rest listen for. And some women who are here present, may know themselves to have the same power. Such women have bright eyes, quick wits, decided ways, rapid tongues. They can't understand why other people should be so slow, any more than the needle can understand why the thread is such a lifeless, helpless, flabby thing. Their words click and dart and flash about faster than the needles themselves, and they are often sharp too, like needles. Some-- times they prick others, sometimes the owner's own fingers.

A quick wit and a ready tongue give very great power for good or evil to the possessor. "A word spoken in due season, how good is it." · Lives have been saved or lost before now in consequence of three or four hastily spoken · words. A friend has been made into an enemy by a smart saying, a nick-name, or a sing-song bit of rhyme.   Saul could bear many far harder trials better than that the women should sing in their songs and dances, "Saul hath slain his thousands, and David his ten thousands."   Most of us would rather be struck than have a proverb. made about us, or a nick-name given to us because of any little deformity or peculiarity we had.   Some people cannot help noticing these things and making satirical remarks about them, or giving sharp clever answers when they are spoken to, which others find it almost impossible to forgive.   The ancients had an expression, "heart-cutting words," which is in no danger, I fear, of becoming old-fashioned, at least, as far as the sense goes.   There is a story told of a clever, but dwarfish and deformed man,* asking his companion, "What is a note of interrogation?" "Oh, a little crooked thing that asks questions!" said the other.   Here you see the pleasure of saying a witty thing tempted him not to mind saying an ill-natured one. , Or sometimes people say unfeeling things, not so much for the sake of being thought clever, as because they really have no sense of what is becoming or considerate. A story is told of a great court lady,† who was

* Alexander Pope, the famous poet.
† Madame de Pompadour.

driving through a town in France, when her carriage ran over a poor old woman. There was a great outcry, for the woman was killed, and a crowd collected round the carriage. "What is the matter?" said she, putting out her head. "Some one killed? Well, there's something to bury her." And she threw some money out of the window, and bade the coachman drive on. The words were perhaps soon forgotten by the speaker, but the nation long remembered them.

Sometimes, on the other hand, a quickly spoken word is of the greatest value for good. About one hundred years ago, a young lady was boasting in the presence of her father's partner, a good man, some years older than herself, of her cleverness in making bargains and saving money. "Ah!" said he, "you are fit to live in the world." She never forgot the lesson those few words had given her, that a spirit of chaffering and money making was a thing not to be boasted of, but rather to be ashamed of and struggled against.* Or, take another instance. There was once a good bishop,† whose brother, though

---

* The speaker will be known to some of our readers as William Stevens, founder of "Nobody's Club," and the honoured friend of Bishop Horne and Jones of Nayland.

† St. Francis de Sales. *(See his Life.)*

possessed of many virtues, had one great fault, that of a very hasty temper. He was an unmarried man. One day, when he had got into a passion about a trifle, the bishop, instead of reproving him, merely said, " Ah brother, I cannot help thinking you have done a great kindness to *one* woman—I mean the woman who *might have been your wife !* "

So you see a quick wit, like a sharp needle, may be a blessing or a curse, according to the hands it is in ; and the power of saying clever things is a talent which will have to be accounted for, and which if any of us have, we should not take foolish pride in, and misemploy, but carefully and prayerfully seek to direct and control.

Do then, my dear friends, remember when you are sitting at work, that the sharpest needle in your huswife is not half so sharp as your own tongue. Your hand flies quickly to and from your work, and your needle flashes backwards and forwards fifty times perhaps in a minute. But what is that to the pace at which your words fly about ? Those words can draw blood, believe me, just as a needle can. And oh, how easy they are to say ! And yet what consequences they leave behind them ! Many of you get into the way of working stitch after stitch so easily, that you would hardly know your needle had been through the calico, if it were not for the bit of thread which remained to tell the tale.

Many of us get into the way of talking, sentence after sentence, so carelessly, that we should not know what we had said unless some one else told us of it. And alas! how much that we say and forget, lingers in the memory of others. An unkind word, rankling like a wound in our neighbour's heart; a wicked word, polluting the minds of one of our innocent little children; an untrue word, that set one of our friends against another; an unholy word, displeasing to Almighty God. These are some of the stitches we put in. Who is to unpick them? Oh, you all know how disheartening it is to unpick a bit of bad work. As we hear you often say, It's far worse than doing it right from the very beginning. Of course it is—and the work has always a pulled, untidy, tumbled look. There is no freshness in it. So with the mischief we have done with our bad words. We may go fumbling about for a long time before we can remedy it. We think we have got hold of a thread, and it turns out to be the wrong one. We strain our eyes and fret our spirits, and we often find this bad work obstinately refuses to come out. "Ah!" we say, "I wish the good things I have done would last half as well as the bad ones!" And not only that, but this melancholy and unsatisfactory process of unpicking takes up all the time we might have had for better things. You know how vexatious it is to spend the best part of an afternoon, picking out a bit of work that you or some one else has done badly—(for alas! we often leave our bad work for others to set straight,) but what is that to the weariness of spirit with which we try to do away the bad effects of our past wrong saying or wrong doing?

Now, if you look in your needle-books, you will see the needles are very unlike one another, just as different people's ways of talking and behaving may be. There is the tall slow-moving darning needle, a patient creature who goes about the world trying to make up for other people's short comings—doing a great deal of homely work, and not going much into company, but very steady and useful. There is another great thick sturdy needle, "almost as big as a skewer," which blurts out what it has got to say like an awkward woman who can't help being downright and straightforward, and whom people trust and make use of, without exactly liking or admiring her. There are the active *eights* and *nines*, who get through their work quickly and cleverly, and can say sharp things when they like. There are the fine little *elevens*, who go about the world whispering in a sly insinuating way, and are fond of having to do with anyone who wears elegant dresses and lace, but have not much power of standing out against anything wrong. Then there are the bodkins, slowest and heaviest of all, very silent, very reserved, neglected in a general way, but *the* people you come to to pull you through a really great difficulty, however long, and dark, and dull, and tiresome the way may be.

Now we cannot settle for ourselves which of these we shall resemble. But if we are heavy and awkward, we must try to make up for it by being sensible and trustworthy. If we are quick and handy, we must take care to be gentle too. If we are delicate and finely made, we must be all the more strict with ourselves, and not let any timidity make us keep back from doing or saying what is right.

Sometime or other the brightest needle drops into a dusty crack and is lost, or snaps and is useless. Some time or other our hands must be motionless, our voice must be silent, but the work abides.   Good or bad, coarse or fine, white or black, there it remains.   A broken needle cannot alter a single stitch it has ever put in.   No more can we, after death, call back our words and their effects.

I speak especially now to those among us who are, what women are generally said to be, quick of speech, bright, active, decided.   They, too, well know the trial, no one else can, of that very quickness of theirs.   They know what it is to be broken-hearted after a hasty speech. They know what it is to be miserable because they have hurt someone's feelings.   What can we say to them, except to ask them to take a lesson from the very needles that are so constantly in their hands?   Their brightness is a gift, their power of talking is a gift, their keenness is a gift.   Only just as it is with the needles, so with them.   It all depends on how it is used. A needle may be like a shrewd disagreeable woman, whom every one is afraid of because of the sharp things she says, or like a bright, kind, lively, clever one, who understands everybody, and helps everybody, and cheers everybody, and who has her quick tongue always under control, and only differs from others who are slower and duller than herself, by her fitness to help, and her willingness to be at the service of everyone who needs her, and by her uncomplaining readiness to spend and be spent for the good of others.

As the pretty verses you have sometimes heard, tell us—

" Woman's quick wit is never at fault,
When she would make others glad."

Think what a gift that quick wit is, and remember what it is given you for, and then I am sure you will agree with me, that you seldom or never read a better lesson out of a printed volume than you may do, even if you don't know your letters, out of your own needle-book.

G

IX.

A HAMMER AND NAILS.

WHEN we are sitting still on a summer's day by the open window, how many sounds come by turns to keep us company! If in the country, the birds and the breezes; if in the town, a confused noise of voices, wheels, street cries, street music, and the rest.

But there is one sound which belongs to both, telling of cheerful activity and steady useful work, the constant sharp reiterated ring of the workman's hammer, be it the carpenter's in his shop, or the builder's in his yard. It is the very music of industry; it tells of peace, prosperity, and progress. There is one hand at least in the world to-day which is well employed, one piece of good work, we hope, going forward; one man earning a respectable, honest, useful livelihood; one happy home, we would gladly think, maintained by that strong, sober, well-trained hand.

What a blessing it is that God has made men and women to take such pleasure in turning out a good bit of work ; a pleasure which those people who buy the work itself afterwards, can only enjoy in a much smaller degree. One hears, for instance, of some great London or Liverpool merchant giving two thousand guineas for a picture ; and this is supposed to give him the enjoyment of the picture, and to recompense the artist for his " trouble" as it is called. But no money will buy for the wealthy man the real pleasure which the painter has had in putting on his reds and blues, in dreaming over those beautiful faces, in colouring that soft sky, those delicate far-off hills, or that clear pebbly mountain brook. The work may have gone from his studio, he may have pocketed his cheque for two thousand guineas, and written a receipt for it ; but the picture will always be his, part of his very self, dear to him almost as one of his children.

So one often thinks in going over some grand hall or palace. There you see splendid carved sideboards, inlaid tables and cabinets, ornamental wainscots, embroidered hangings, richly wrought gold and silver cups and salvers. Who got the real pleasure out of them ? The lord and lady, who were supposed to be their owners, and who glance at them perhaps now and then, or the poor man or woman who spent days and weeks putting their hearts and hands, their skill, their eyesight, almost one might say their very selves, into the piece of work which so often since has stood neglected, in one of the state apartments of the palace? Surely, the poor work people.

Therefore, let any one who is able to work thank God for his head and his hands, and the power of using them; and, remember above all things, that they are not his own, but lent him for a time, and that he is but a steward of them.

Many people who would at once allow that having money is a gift from God and not due to a man's own merits, are less ready to see that those gifts which we have *in ourselves* are also from God.

A man's fortune does not seem a part of himself in the way that his brains and fingers are. "Banks may break, ships may go down," such an one may exclaim, "but *my* bank is *here.*" And perhaps he puts out his strong right hand as much as to say, "I defy anyone to take *that* from me." And this is why there is often so much conceit about clever working men; they feel that if they were set down in a strange place with only, as we say, "the clothes they stand up in," they would be able to make their way, and pay their way. "Put a tool into my hand," they say, "and the rest will take care of itself." "I have got a head on my shoulders and need not be beholden to anybody," perhaps another man thinks.

Now, of course, there is a common enough way of answering this, and a very true one, to remind them that there are such things as accidents, sickness, insanity, loss of faculties, and old age. But to-day, as we stand in imagination, looking on at a workman with his hammer in his hand, and listening to the music of his strokes, I should like to ask him whether those very tools he uses may not themselves have a meaning which does not meet the eye, an inner voice no less distinct and clear than those regular melodious beats of his ringing tool.

Some who read this paper may have seen a famous picture, lately painted, of our Lord in the carpenter's shop at Nazareth, surrounded by all the tools and implements which carpenters use, and represented as one who works and does not disdain the humblest labour, and tastes weariness like ourselves. This is a most beautiful thought for all who toil for their daily bread, that our Lord and Master set them an example of so doing, and that for a much longer time than the three years and a half of His public ministry. From twelve years of age till thirty we are told nothing of our blessed Saviour ; for more than half of His whole earthly life we know nothing of Him, except that he was subject to Joseph and Mary, at Nazareth. There is nothing to show that He was otherwise employed than in helping Joseph in his daily labours. The Church has loved to imagine Him so employed, condescending to work with tools of man's invention, to bear in His own divine person the curse upon Adam at the fall, " In the sweat of thy face shall thou eat bread."

And yet there is some danger in our dwelling too much on such pictures as these. There is another side to the history which no painter can represent. He may be able to show us Jesus Christ working in the carpenter's shop as man ; but how can he remind us that—as has been beautifully said—the very Being who deigned to labour in this narrow and toilsome sphere, is also the great God who spread out the heavens and laid the foundations of the earth ? The universe is His workshop, all it contains are His materials, created by Him at first, and for ever being sustained and preserved or shaped anew, and wondrously perfected by His will and wisdom. Aye, and both men and nations are, but instruments in His hands, formed for His purposes, ennobled by His use, cast aside if we dare to exalt ourselves against Him. "How is the hammer of the whole earth cut asunder and broken! how is Babylon become a desolation among the nations!" said Jeremiah: l, 23. Or again, "Shall the axe boast itself against him that heweth therewith? or shall the saw magnify himself against him that shaketh it? as if the rod should shake itself against them that lift it up, or as if the staff should lift up itself, as if it were no wood:" Isa. x, 15.*

How surprised any workman would be if the tools in his hand were to resist him. If the hammer instead of coming sharp down on the nail were to swerve aside and fly in his face. He would not go on long patiently with such a tool as that, but would throw it away and get a better. Yet we are perpetually swerving aside from our duties, and too often flying in the face

* Compare Rom. vi, 13: "Yield your members as instruments [tools] of righteousness unto God."

of God's providence.   And still He bears with us.

Every tool too, in the workshop, has its proper use.   There are the common ones that we all know, hammers, saws, planes, chisels, and so on, and a great many less common ones, of which you would have to teach the names, and explain the use, to anybody who did not understand the business of carpenter's or joiner's work.   But the most ignorant person can see at once that an awl will not do the work of a chisel, nor a circular saw that of a hammer, and that every tool is fitted for its special work.   And yet, sometimes, in God's great workshop, men who would be excellent and useful if they minded their own business, fret because they are not placed in some entirely different station, and are restless till they fulfil—not their duty, but their ambition—in some state of life to which it did *not* please God to call them.   Depend upon it, that is not the way for good work to be done. Perhaps you know what it was when you were boys, how you were always trying—say, to wrench open a lid, or to bore a hole, or to do something else for which you had no proper tool, with the blade of one unfortunate pocket-knife.   No wonder if it got jagged and blunted, no wonder if at last the poor thing snapped in half, and left nothing in your hand but a square silly-looking stump half-an-inch long. Poor old misused knife-blade! It was a very good emblem of all those who try to do work out of their proper sphere; it will never even be able to cut a knot or to sharpen a pencil again. So a man who tries to do what he is not fit for, ceases to be fit to do anything, even the smallest matter, as it ought to be done, and as God meant him to do it.

Listen for a moment! There is the ringing of the ever-busy hammer; tap, tap, tap, or clink, clink, clink, it goes on, steadily, busily, cheerfully; knocking up a scaffold perhaps for the spectators of some merry making; industriously employed on some of the fittings or furniture of a house, helping to make a box, a packing case, a door, or a thousand other things.

A merry sound truly and one full of life, and yet how closely associated in our minds with death!

People say sometimes, speaking of a great sorrow, "It is another nail driven into my coffin." How many of those nails have been driven into *our* coffins by the hand of grief, of disappointment, of ingratitude, of pain, of fear, or of misfortune? How many have we helped to drive in for ourselves by our own vices, follies, and sins? How many may we at this very moment be driving in for others? Ah! there is an ungrateful son. He has a hammer in his hand. How many nails is he driving into his mother's coffin? Day and night the strokes keep falling. Now it is a cold look, now a cruel word, now selfish waste of the small means that might have comforted her old age, now he is away from home, and week by week goes by and he never writes to her, now she hears of him drinking, swearing, keeping bad company. The nails are sharp, the strokes are true, the wood is yielding. The coffin is nearly ready, and when she is laid in it he will perhaps be the first to weep over the old, soft, pure, tender face, as he looks on it for the last time, and even then perhaps he will wonder what it was that killed her.

Still we hear it ringing, ringing evermore, the sound of the hammer. It is like a passing bell that never stops. It seems to say "Yes, O man, you think I am your tool, your servant, and yet the time will come when I shall be more than your master; Your hand will be no more able to lift me, your head will be no more able to direct me. I shall help to make ready for you your last abiding place. You will not be able to resist. As you wield me now you are whistling tunes or singing ballads at your work. You will be silent then, nor able to raise your voice to accompany my repeated strokes ; your working apron will be laid by, and you clothed in your shroud ; your labours will all be done. The bell will never call you out to work again, or send you home at night. No ! but there is .the church-bell calling to' your funeral. So, farewell. I am but dead wood and cold iron, and yet I am longer lived than you, with all your pride of skill and strength of arm."

Alas ! alas ! for the sound of the hammer. Could we always think of its message to us, we should take no such pride in our work, no more should we boast ourselves of the power, the knowledge, the ability, that we are now so fond of displaying.

On the other hand, if this were all, we should be likely to fall into the opposite extreme, to let our hands lie idle, and to say with Solomon : " What hath man of all his labour, and of the vexation of his heart wherein he hath laboured under the sun ? I have seen all the works that are done under the sun, and behold, all is vanity and vexation of' spirit."

Can the thought of death be constantly present with us without its taking all the heart, all the energy, all the spirit for work out of our lives? Is there anything that will make death seem less terrible to us?

Let us go back once more to the hammer and nails we were speaking of before. We sometimes see those nails represented in our churches, together with the spear and the crown of thorns, as emblems of our Lord's passion. Singular it is, how one by one as we follow up the leading ideas of life, they almost all seem to be brought to a head, as it were, in that wonderful history. As if the death of Christ were to radiate through the whole circle of our lives, and as if the whole circle of our lives were to be gathered up there, as the rays are in the sun.

We have seen our Lord, the divine Maker of heaven and earth, figuring that higher office by his labour in the workshop with Joseph, at Nazareth. We now see Him, at the close of His earthly ministry, submitting to have those very materials, with and upon which He once worked turned against Him, to have those very hands with which He had laboured now nailed to the wood of the cross. Wonderful image, of the world, His great creation, of man, His noblest implement,

turning against their Master and their Maker;
while He Himself, condescends to be subjected
for a time to the power of brute force, of dull
matter, of dead dry wood, and of hard, cold,
lifeless iron.   As we think of this it seems to take
our breath away.   What! will our Lord submit His
Body to be, in one sense, not only subject to the
power of man, but something at the mercy of the
inanimate, the soulless, the heartless, the speech-
less, and the senseless?   Aye, He has indeed
done so, that you and I, and we all, may no
longer dread the time when, as it seems, we too
must fall a prey to death, must be domineered
over by the basest things of earth, shut in between
the boards of our coffins, fastened down by nails
and screws of iron, and buried in a darkness
deep as that which brooded over Calvary.
Aye, He has done so; and more than that,
He bears about for ever in His glorified Body,
the print of the nails, the wound of the spear,
the proofs of His resurrection, the pledges of
our own.   As He said to Thomas, He says now
to us, "Be not faithless, but believing."

The iron and the wood of the cross have
hallowed the iron and the wood of our coffins.
If we would only remember Christ in our work,
Christ will be with us in our death.   If we,

would only work, not for ourselves, but for Him and His, we should have no fear when our work was over, and the familiar tools dropped from our hands, and all was silence in our quiet sick-rooms. If we would think of ourselves as His implements, and acknowledge Him as our master, then all our labours would be blessed.

We should work not for time, but for eternity. The houses we had built, the furniture we had made, all the offspring of our heads and hands might perish, and yet our work, our real work, would remain ; and it would be said of us, as it was of the saints of old, " Blessed are the dead which die in the Lord ; even so, saith the Spirit, for they rest from their labours, and their works do follow them."

X.

A HOARDING.

THIS is to be a paper for Londoners, or people
who live in some other large town.   There have
been so many beautiful things said about trees
and flowers, birds, and other country sights, that
surely it is time we Cockneys had our turn.
Those of us who have spent many long years
among the chimney-pots, have learnt to love our
foggy, smoky, noisy London, as warmly as other
people do blue skies and green fields.   And I
am sure if we do not find, as we go about the
streets and look in at the shop windows, many
things to teach us useful lessons, it will have
been our own fault.

You know, of course, what is meant by a
hoarding.   The barricade that is put up round
any place where building is to be carried on.
Perhaps some dilapidated old ruined sheds
have to be pulled down, and one or more
handsome new houses to be erected in their

place.   But the hoarding is put up, and we do
not see much of what goes on behind it, for
the boards are high, and the street is too
narrow to let us get far away.   There is a little
rough wooden door, and "No admittance except
on business," painted on it.   Early and late men
in dusty fustian coats come and go through this
door.   Of course those are the workmen who
are to build the house.   Bricks and stones, and
ropes and planks, and other things necessary for
their work were taken in by them, though
nothing was much out of the common way, so
far as we could see.   But the hoarding—*that*
really is worth looking at!   So think the little
boys and girls as they pass it on their way to
school.   It is like a great picture book, with new
pictures nearly every day.   One day it is a
staring portrait of a gentleman with a blue coat
and a white tie, and a never-ceasing grin on his
face—Mr. Reginald Augustus de Montmorency—
the celebrated comic singer.   Another day it is
a large bull's head, on the top of an advertise-
ment about mustard.   Next time it is a rather
melancholy representation of a man walking in
the rain, with a patent umbrella and patent
waterproof.   You can see the rain coming down
in slanting black lines, and dropping from all

the points of his umbrella. He is looking round at us over his shoulder with a smile, as if trying to say how much he liked it. Then perhaps there will be a lady with one side of her head grey and one yellow, or brushing her hair with great industry, to show that people never need have their hair fall off or turn white, if they use somebody's dye, or somebody else's magnetic brush. Or there will be a man riding three horses at once, or a grand torchlight scene of a robbers' cavern at the theatre, or some other interesting and wonderful picture ; only, unluckily, now and then these pictures get others pasted over them, or are torn or blown away, or spattered with mud. However, what *does* it matter, when there is sure to be something fresh to-morrow ?

Besides that, there are all sorts of printed papers of many colours, with blue, red, and yellow letters, a most distracting variety. To say nothing of the notices of sermons, and tea-meetings, which are generally rather small, and in black, and perhaps catch the eye more on that account. Gay or grave, comic or serious, amusing or instructive, all have their turn. Each has its readers, each its day, sometimes perhaps its week. And then another broadsheet comes and hides all of its predecessor, except a

H

little ragged pink edge that still flaps in the wind, till the next bill-sticker tears it off.

Hundreds of people stop to look at the bills and pictures on this hoarding. Hardly any one tries to find out about the house behind it. Indeed they could not very easily peep through the cracks, for most of them have been pasted over. Any one who listened might, however, hear the tinkle of the workmen's trowels, or the sound of their voices, or might see them wheeling different things in through the door. But the building goes on, like most great works, quietly, steadily, and secretly.

At last the set day comes, the hoarding is taken down, the rubbishy bits of paper torn off, and lo! there is a palace behind, fit for a king! Grand marble pillars, carved capitals, beautiful pierced iron work, large plate-glass windows shining in the sun are there. The old miserable hovels are gone. Everything is new, fresh, and splendid, and looks as if it would last for ever. And this magnificent palace has grown up close to us, while we were only paying attention to the red and yellow bits of trashy paper plastered on the tumble-down old hoarding outside.

By this time you will have perhaps guessed the application to be made of this little story.

Each one of us may have a palace built up within him, (our very word to edify—though used in a spiritual sense—means to build up.) And for whom is this palace to be raised in our souls? Surely, you will say, for the King of Kings. Can it be built in a day? Certainly not. It must take a whole lifetime. Can any one see it being built? No. The kingdom of God cometh not with observation. The kingdom of God is within you.

But outside this palace, outside our inner spiritual life, there is another life, which every passer-by can see. The workmen within may be doing their duty, or, on the other hand, they may be wasting or misusing their time. The hoarding outside tells no tales. So a man may be trying to fit his soul to be the dwelling of God, or he may be taking no pains with himself. His outer life very likely tells no tales.

Some things come to good and bad people alike. They live apparently almost the same lives. The outward shows of one day succeed the outward shows of another, just as the circus dancer was pasted over the comic singer. The surface of life keeps changing. We have our buying and selling, our amusements, our eating and drinking, our walking and talking, our railway travelling perhaps, and our church-going, and these things come one after another, just as the pictures and notices of them did on the hoarding. But who, from these, can judge of the state of our souls—of our inner life? As little could a man do so, as pronounce how a building was getting on, without stepping behind the barricade.

Two lives might be written of every man or woman. One by a brother man, the other by an angel. One would, doubtless, say how many years he lived, how much money he had, how he got on in his business, whether he had a family, what his health was, and so on. The other would say how far he progressed in the ways of holiness, what faults he conquered, what prayers he prayed, what kind actions he did, how often he denied himself, what good he did in secret, what yearnings he had for a holier nature. One of these lives would be like the hoarding, the other like the palace. One would represent the *real man*, the other his common-place every day outside, that which a few years would destroy and do away with for ever, while the first would remain to all eternity

I have said that the workmen went to and fro very quietly. The bricks and stones and all the other materials had nothing about them to catch the eye. There was nothing gaudy, nothing showy, nothing pretentious. So the building up of our souls is a quiet, regular work. It does not catch the eye. For what is that spiritual life made up of? Short, fervent, silent prayers, quiet kindnesses, secret self-denials, patient, and often dull and hard work—one day like another. Alms-giving, when our left hand knows not what our right hand doeth. Fasting, which only He that seeth in secret is able to discern. Battles with ourselves, which the world will never be made aware of. Endeavours after holiness as slow, as steady, as quiet, as regular, as course after course of brickwork, laid by some careful mason, on deep, underground foundations. But who would not derive more benefit and satisfaction from a single brick or stone so carefully laid, than from all the gaudy trumpery plastered up outside?

Well, at last the house is finished. The scaffolding is taken down. Perhaps a garland is placed on the roof, or a flag set flying. The master is coming. There is great rejoicing. He is welcomed perhaps with song and music. For it is his house. The workmen were but labourers in his employ; their time was at his disposal.

Every brick, every stone, was his property. The land it was built on was his.

So it is with God's dwelling in our souls. A time will come when the builder's work is finished, when all is complete, and the temporary outside is done away with. Such times come to us all. And strangely are we often surprised to see in the case of others what a noble palace God has been building up behind a poor outside. When people die their good comes out. We see a woman, "a good sort of person," as we say, who has been generally rather looked down upon. She dies, and then we find we have had an angel beside us unawares. So many little tokens of thoughtfulness, so many tender words, so much unobtrusive piety, such gentle unselfishness. These were the bricks of her house. Mere earth, and yet what a house it is! What a character, what an example she has left! When shall we see any one like her again? O that we ourselves were like her. And yet we may be sure such persons never take any credit to themselves. All the good they have done is God's doing, not theirs. He has been building them up, by the grace of His Holy Spirit. "Not unto us, O Lord," they would say, "not unto us, but unto thy name be the praise."

But we must remember that there are houses which never get finished, but which are left in a miserable state of faultiness and incompleteness. When the day comes which had been fixed upon it is found that the contractor has not half done his work. There has been no pains taken, the foundations have been ill-laid, the walls are beginning to give way, the wood-work is shrinking, the bricks were hastily made and show signs of scaling off already. The stones have been left lying about the yard the wrong way upwards, and the wet has penetrated into them and begun to decay them. The floors are uneven. There is not a door that opens and shuts well, the bolts are rusty, the roof not water-tight, the glass of the windows makes everything seem crooked that is seen through it. Great streaks of damp are appearing on the walls and rising up through the stones of the kitchen and passages. The workmen have been idle and dishonest. All has gone wrong. There stands the house, a gaping, useless, blank, un-furnished, and utterly forlorn tenement. The master, be sure, will never live there. It must be pulled down, its very foundations must be removed, and its site made use of for another house, built by some more trustworthy contractor.

Meanwhile it is a mockery, a failure, a disappointment. Thieves and murderers may take refuge within it, vermin may harbour there, but nothing good, nothing happy, nothing noble, can find a home there.

Are any of us letting our spiritual house—God's dwelling-place—thus miserably to go to ruin? Every day wasted makes it harder to repair the breaches, to build aright on the foundation, which perhaps itself is all wrongly laid. Remember, you are like contractors, who have to get your work finished by a particular day. That day is drawing very near. Why, then, are the workmen so idle? Why are the materials so carelessly used? From time to time the Great Master comes and looks, not as the world looks—on the hoarding outside, but on the progress of the house itself. God looks into our hearts, to see if we are trying by communion with Him to make them fit for His abode. Can we truly say we *are* trying? Can we truly say we *are* making ready for the day of reckoning? Will our house be fit for Him?

The husband cannot tell of his wife. The mother cannot tell of her children. None of us can tell of the other. We can see the hoarding, but not the house. But God can

see within. Do let us ask Him to help us to be
in earnest. If we were only half as earnest as we
should be about a new house or cottage that was
being built for us, it would be something. Oh,
dear friends, would that any one had words to
make us feel even for a moment the unspeakable
consequence of this great, this silent, this daily
and hourly work, this work that is to last for
ever and evermore!

Come, O Thou great Master-builder, to the
house which is being made ready for Thee.
Cleanse it from all that is unclean and unworthy.
Fill it with Thy glory. Drive far from it all the
powers of sin and darkness, and make it wholly
Thine. " Behold, the tabernacle of God is with
men, and he will dwell with them, and they shall
be his people, and God himself shall be with
them, and be their God."

May He, indeed, so dwell in us and with us,
for evermore! And to that end may He help
us all now by patient and faithful labour, to fit
ourselves for nearer and more intimate communion with Him, both here and hereafter.

XI.

A DEAL BOARD.

FROM some cause or another, we find ourselves to-night in a perfectly empty room. It may be the waiting-room of a small station, or of some gentleman's office, or some other place, where we have to spend half-an-hour very much against our will with nothing to do. There is no furniture in the room, except a perfectly plain deal table, made evidently at the smallest possible outlay of time, and money, and trouble, just like a kitchen dresser, only not quite so large. It does not at first seem a fruitful subject for meditation, however, we find ourselves studying it, and wondering about it in an idle way. We observe the veins and marks that run all over it, we see how the tree from which it was made must have grown, we begin perhaps to guess the age of the tree. We notice the little dark knots, where the branches started off from the parent stem—we can fancy the direction in which they must have sprung—and a little imagination helps us to cover them with stiff needle-like leaves, and even to see a squirrel perched among them. In fact, though the tree has long ago been sawn into planks, it still continues to tell its story. We may chop the wood up into any shape we please, but we cannot alter a single vein or knot in it. As long as it has any being at all, it must be *itself*. It cannot turn, for instance, into a bit of oak, or walnut-wood. Deal it was, and deal it will be, to the end of time.

Now, of course, it would have been waste of breath to trouble you with saying all this, unless something could be drawn from it as regarded ourselves. And surely you will grant that much may be so drawn forth. *We* are the real deal boards; or, if you do not think that comparison good enough, oak, birch, ash, mahogany, what you will. We may be cut and planed, and shaped and polished in a variety of ways; we may be presented to the world's gaze under manifold forms, and appear in several characters at the same time to different persons, and yet we shall never lose what is called our personal identity— our self-sameness. We cannot turn into another person. We can alter our dress, our language, our way of living, but we cannot, in this sense alter ourselves. John or William may go up to London, make a large fortune, and come back riding in his own carriage, but he continues to be the same John or William through it all. And he is so well aware of this that he very likely avoids the company of those who knew him when he was a poor lad, because he does not like them to notice those little points which somehow he cannot get over. He may have learnt to be particular about his grammar and his h's, but he can't alter the tone of his voice, or the little peculiar movements of his mouth and eyes, which he inherited from his grandfather. He may have got a fashionable coat, but he cannot change the cut of his features. He may have got hundreds of pounds where he used to have half-pence, but he cannot turn his thin lanky hair into thick curling locks. A man may carry out a new line of railway, nay more, he may alter the boundaries of an empire, and yet not be able to change the shape of a single wrinkle on his own face. And as with the body, so with the faculties of the mind. A clever man cannot make himself stupid, a slow man cannot (except in some small degree) make himself quick, a dull man cannot become imaginative, a man with no ear cannot become a good musician.

But we must distinguish between the faculties of the mind, and the qualities of the soul. A bad man may, thank God, become a good one, an idle man a hard working one, and so on. But he does not become a *different person.* Whatever else is changed about us, we can never become, as was said before, anyone but ourselves. People sometimes try to persuade themselves that they can do so, that after death they melt away into the universe as a drop of rain water melts in a river. But this is not only a false, but a mischievous notion, because it destroys men's belief in a judgment to come, and in rewards and punishments after death. Job knew better. He said, " I know that my Redeemer liveth, and that he shall stand at the latter day upon the earth, and though after my skin worms destroy this body, yet in my flesh shall I see God : whom I shall see for myself, and mine eyes shall behold, and *not another.*"

What it is that makes what we call *self* is a very hard question, and one which often puzzles people who are not Christians. But those who study their Bibles cannot doubt that the doctrine we are speaking of is often repeated in it. Moses was the same Moses, Elias the same Elias, at the Transfiguration, as they had been hundreds

of years before.   People sometimes say that the
whole substance of the body is changed in the
course of seven years, and try to persuade us
that something of the same kind is true of the
soul.   But if this were so, how could there be
any justice in God's punishments, overtaking
offenders after a long lapse of years, as we know
from Scripture that they do?

But to return again for a moment to our "deal
board."   The grains and veins in a piece of
wood seem to resemble so closely the peculiari-
ties of a man's character, that we actually use
the expression "against the grain" in this very
sense.   And let us pursue the thought not any
longer with this plain deal table, but with the
beautiful wood carvings in a palace or a church.

Can anything be more exquisite than the
garlands of carved leaves, and flowers, and fruit,
or the beautiful figures we see sometimes in a
church or cathedral?   And yet we see just the
same thing *there* as we do in our plain deal table.
You cannot get rid of the grain of the wood.   Yet
it does not interfere with the carving, but rather
enriches it, and gives softness and variety to it.
Now is there not a very striking suggestion contained in this?   We hope, some day, to be part
of the heavenly city and temple, of which our

Lord is the corner-stone, and the apostles and prophets are the foundation. We hope to rise again with glorified bodies and sanctified souls.

People have often been puzzled and unhappy at the thought that perhaps in another world they will not know their friends again. They will be so altered. How can we, with all our faults and weaknesses, ever hope to be *ourselves*, and yet to be part of the heavenly temple? And yet we see it is so. There is the grain of the wood showing itself through all the turnings and windings of the scroll-work, and all the intricacies of branch, leaf, and blossom, of carved shaft-work, and wreathed capital. So with all the innocent characteristics of those we love. Why should they cease in another world? When God has given us so much of the beauty of character and individuality here, why should we think He will not do so hereafter? Again, why must we believe that the past will be entirely blotted out? A piece of wood still bears the impress of the time when it grew in the forest. Why should we forget the days of our spiritual growth and struggle in this life?

[No ignorant person, looking at a tree as it grows, would be able to guess what a number of things could be made out of it, and to how many uses it might be turned.   So, in a certain sense, it may be with us.   Hereafter, each of us will be but *one person*, but who can tell how *many powers* may be brought to light in us?   *Here* we have but five senses, and can only move slowly from place to place, and in many other ways feel as if our understanding and all our faculties were imperfect and undeveloped.   *There*, who can tell but that we may travel as swiftly as our own thoughts, and have many roads to knowledge opened to us, beside those of sight, hearing, and the like?   New ways of serving, knowing, and enjoying God, of learning heavenly wisdom, of practising divine love.]*

In a certain way the cutting down of a tree seems like death.   And very melancholy are the thoughts which such a sight suggests to us, if we pause there and go no further.   We feel the tree has had its last chance; that henceforth it will have no opportunities of growing to any greater height, of putting forth any fresh shoots, of becoming any better than it is.   Such a sight gives us most impressively a sense of irrevocableness, of life that can never be called back.   What

* This passage, within brackets, may be omitted if too difficult.

a warning it is to us to profit by the time that is still left to us.*

Perhaps we have sometimes noticed in a wood, or an avenue, a tree with a red mark on the stem. "Ah," we say, "that means that tree will have to come down." Perhaps we have sometimes left a sick room, sighing, as we closed the street door, "Ah, that poor man is not long for this world. He is like a tree with the woodman's mark upon him.† Death has his axe ready sharpened, and has even now his hand raised to strike the first blow." Perhaps we may feel ourselves like a fated tree with only a few days or hours of life before us. So it once was with the cedars of Lebanon; Hiram's woodman may have marked them, and then the fatal day came, and they were laid low, with a crash as of thunder,

---

* We find an ancient poet using this very image to express a determination that cannot be altered. The speaker is a warrior, who has been deeply injured by his commander-in-chief. "Sooner," he says, "shall this dead staff in my hand, which has been hewn down by the woodman's axe, put forth fresh shoots and buds, than I be persuaded to change my mind, and forgive him who has wronged me." And with that he flung his staff angrily down on the ground.

† "Like crowded forest trees we stand,
    And some are marked to fall ;
   The axe will smite at God's command,
    And soon shall smite us all."—*Cowper.*

I

and the glory of their evergreen crown was torn and levelled with the earth. But was that the end? We know it was rather the beginning of a new, and holier, and better life. Theirs was to be the golden splendour of the temple, the glory of God's presence, the voice of worship, the prayer of Solomon, the hymns and psalms of the inspired poets and musicians. This is no new thought; we see it in the grand xxixth Psalm, uttered by David as a prophecy; a Psalm used by the Jewish Church on the day of Pentecost. It first speaks of the glory of one of those sublime mountain storms. "The voice of the LORD is upon the waters: the God of glory thundereth: the LORD is upon many waters. . . . The voice of the LORD breaketh the cedars; yea, the LORD breaketh the cedars of Libanus." And then at the end our thoughts are turned to these same cedars, no longer growing on the wild mountain-top, but in the sacred and calm temple of God. "In His temple, everything cries Glory." (*See marginal note in the Bible.*)

So we see in Isaiah's wonderful vision, the very posts of the house trembled at the divine presence: (Isaiah vi, 4,) and at the angelic cry, "Holy, holy, holy, is the LORD of hosts, the whole earth is full of His glory." What a blessed anticipation this gives us of what may be in store for God's saints in the world to come. Here there are the storms—there are the hallelujahs. Here is the wind shaking our branches and threatening to uproot us—there is the heavenly breath of sacred song. Here is death putting his mark upon us, in disease, sorrow, and old age, and sharpening his axe to fell us to earth— *there* is life and immortality, and the presence of God. O may it be ours, ere long, to behold that presence, and to echo back that cry, " Holy, holy, holy, is the LORD of hosts : heaven and earth are full of the majesty of his glory." Amen.

XII.

A CUP.

———

SOME, very likely most of us, have known what it is to be recovering from a bad illness, when the pain is pretty nearly gone, and yet we are so weak that we can hardly speak or move, and feel that if any body were to set us off laughing or crying, we should never be able to stop ourselves. Perhaps we have been amused at the way we can go on looking at some bit of furniture in the room, or some trifle that nobody else ever thought of noticing, and the quantity of interest we can find in it.

Our *well* friends, we feel, would laugh at us if we told them half the fancies we had about the pattern of a curtain, the leg of a table, or the bit of red tiled roof we could see from our window. And yet, till we have lain hour after hour looking at things of this kind, we can never know how much there is in the dullest trifle to set us off thinking.

Suppose now that you or I are lying ill in bed—I am sure I hope it is only a "suppose," and will not for many a long day be a reality-- but *suppose* we are. There is the clock ticking and the fire crackling and the window rattling. People's voices are heard coming up indistinctly through the floor. Opposite us is a table with our bottle of physic and a drinking cup and a book. We have taken our physic, and don't want to think about *that* any more, thank you, for the next three hours. No one is near to read to us, and our eyes and hands are far too weak for us to try to read ourselves. So we are left to look at the drinking cup; a bit of plain common crockery, with only a flowery pink pattern round the edge, just such a piece of earthenware as you may buy any day for a few pence. Earthenware, made of earth, of clay, mixed and kneaded up smooth, shaped on a wheel, painted and baked and glazed, packed in straw, and then sold to us.

As we say the words they seem almost like an echo of the Bible, "The Lord God formed man of the dust of the ground," says the book of Genesis. "Remember, I beseech thee, that thou hast made me as the clay; and wilt thou bring me into dust again?" says Job, pleading with God: x, 9. And Isaiah says: lxiv, 8, "But now, O LORD, thou art our father; we are the clay, and thou our potter; and we all are the work of thy hand."

I suppose there is nothing that gives us such a feeling of the power one being has over another, as the power we have over a handful of clay, to shape it as we like. We see it even in the little children making mud pies by the roadside; those small fingers and little brains are learning a lesson which they will soon apply to things of more consequence. What was a mere lump of earth, the dullest clod one minute ago, may turn out something beautiful and useful to last for years; long, perhaps, after the hands that made it shall themselves have crumbled to dust.

If we go to any places where old curiosities are kept, we shall find fragments of earthenware, hundreds and even thousands of years old. Two lumps of clay may have lain in the same heap in the potter's yard side by side. One may have been trodden down into the mire and soon forgotten, and the other may have fallen into the hands of some good workman, and been made into a beautiful cup or plate, which now-a-days you could not buy, as the saying is, "for any money." How exactly this is like what St. Paul says, " Hath not the potter power over the clay, of the same lump to make one vessel unto honour, and another unto dishonour? Shall the thing formed say unto him that formed it, Why hast thou made me thus?" Rom. ix, 20, 21.

We have no doubt that there are few greater trials to any one, man or woman, than bodily deformity or weakness. To be crooked when other people are straight, to have anything wrong with one's eyes or features, to be lame when others are able and active, or to be in any way ugly or unsightly is, even to sensible people, a great mortification. We cannot help liking health and beauty better than their contraries, and it does seem hard, very hard, to be deprived of what our fellow creatures enjoy. It is just like the earthenware vessels. A common and badly shaped bit of red crockery or yellow Delft is one thing, a fine delicate piece of eggshell china, or a lovely Greek vase, another. But we must be thankful to our Creator for giving us *any* kind of being. The most sickly and feeble frame among us is a great deal better than none at all, just as the poorest and commonest bit of earthenware is a great deal better than a mere shapeless lump of clay.

· There is a story told of a learned man, who was once called upon to preach before the Pope. It was usual for preachers to do this on their knees. The Pope, however, bade him rise. He was so short that the Pope thought he was kneeling, when he was in reality standing, and bade him a second time to rise. In some amazement, the good man—(a really wise as well as learned one)—when he saw the Pope's surprise, modestly observed in the words of the Psalm, "It is he that hath made us, and not we ourselves."*

If we could all look on our poor bodies of clay with such a feeling as this, we should never murmur, however it might please God to afflict us through them, and however little form or comeliness they had to the eye of man. Man looketh only on the outward appearance, but the Lord looketh on the heart.

But let us glance at our drinking cup again. It has got something good and wholesome in it.

* *Beatissime Pater, ipse fecit nos, et non ipsi nos.* This anecdote will be found in the Life of Cornelius à Lapide, the famous commentator on Scripture.

Milk, very likely. The physic bottle, of course. has physic ; the jug on the shelf, perhaps, has beef-tea ; the brown crock on the floor has water. Now, not one of these vessels had any choice given it as to what was to be poured into it. Is not this also like ourselves ? We have all got gifts of mind as well as of body—cleverness, quickness, good taste, memory, good temper, cheerfulness, and so forth. Things we cannot *make*, but which are *poured into* us, just as the different drinks are into different cups. Now how very foolish it would be if the milk jug were to say to the water jug, " Oh! I'm a great deal better than you, because I have got what is far superior inside me." When we know pefectly well that it is due to no worth of its own, but all depends on what happened to be poured into it. And yet how we pride ourselves on our gifts, which God could take away from us in a moment, and more easily than you or I could pour the milk or water out of one of those jugs. None of us are gifted as St. Paul was, but what did he say, " We have this treasure in earthen vessels, that the excellency of the power may be of God, and not of us:" 2 Cor. iv, 7.

But can we remain quite dull and passive,

and make no use of God's good gifts? Surely
not. We shall have to give an account of them all,
and must not therefore let them, as it were, turn
sour and grow corrupt in our keeping. If you pour
anything into a cup that has not been properly
cleansed it will spoil, and become unwholesome
and be wasted. So it is with God's good
gifts poured into a corrupt and impure heart.
Everything tastes bad out of an unclean vessel.

Nor must we be like cracked or leaky vessels,
and let the good that is in us run to waste·
What does St. Paul say to Timothy? " Neglect
not the gift that is in thee:" 1 Timothy iv, 14.
And again, speaking of false doctrine: 2 Tim.
ii, 20; " But in a great house there are not only
vessels of gold and of silver, but also of wood
and of earth, and some to honour, and some to
dishonour. "If a man, therefore, purge himself
from these, he shall be a vessel unto honour,
sanctified, and meet for the master's use, and
prepared unto every good work:" Such were
St. Paul's words—himself God's chosen vessel.
So we see plainly our own duty, to pray to God
for grace to keep the vessels of our own hearts
pure, and to show us what use we can make of
them for His service.

One thing more. You all know how shocked

we cannot help being when a cup is dashed to the ground, the water spilt, and the cup itself shattered to pieces. It gives one a picture of destruction which no words could. At Jewish weddings a cup is broken over the head of the bride and bridegroom to show the frailty of all earthly joy. Some feeling of the same kind hung about a celebrated drinking-glass, treasured in an old family in Cumberland, and it was believed that the luck of the house depended on this cup being preserved—

> " If this glass either break or fall,
>   Then farewell the luck of Edenhall."

Man's life, we know, is like water spilt on the ground which cannot be gathered up again. An accident, a fit of passion, a slip of hand or foot, and the beautiful cup—a moment ago brimful of sweetnesses—lies shattered on the ground, and all that was in it is spilt and wasted. How like, O how strangely like a sudden death! "Thou shalt dash them in pieces like a potter's vessel," says King David, speaking of God's vengeance on His enemies.

But do you not remember one wonderful passage in Bible history, where the breaking of a potter's vessel produced quite a different effect?

In Judges vii, we read of Gideon, the leader of Israel against the Midianites, and how he took three hundred men and put a trumpet into every man's hand, with empty pitchers, and lamps within the pitchers, and how they came on their enemies by night, and at a signal from him blew the trumpets, and brake the pitchers that were in their hands, crying "The sword of the Lord and of Gideon;" and how they thus surprised and overthrew their enemies. What a sight it must have been when those three hundred torches suddenly flashed out upon the darkness. But was this deed to end with the defeat of the Midianites? Was it not rather to be a figure to all mankind of what will happen hereafter to God's true servants? Their bodies are like the earthen pitchers, shattered by death; but O how beautifully then does the bright and fiery soul shine forth! It seems as if it had been before like a prisoner in a confined and choked-up cell, but was now darting forth to light, and air, and freedom. Have we never seen such a death-bed, when the inner light of holiness shone brighter and brighter as the poor walls of clay were battered and impaired, and as the outward man perished the inward man was renewed day by day? We all know that look of heavenly hope that comes over a dying face—all know, too well, that unearthly smile; those words that seem like wandering, and yet tell of the only real world—the world beyond the darkness of the grave; we know that cry for " more light ; " we know that peaceful and happy smile, the sunrise-gleam that comes in its perfect beauty on the face of one just departed. So may it be given to us in God's good time to "depart and be with Christ, which is far better."

Here we might pause, but other thoughts come crowding in, one especially, namely, of the alabaster box of precious ointment which the woman brake and poured on our Lord's head. Alabaster is a fine white delicate substance, something like white marble, only softer. It seems like purity itself, not merely with a glaze of white on the surface as your clay drinking cup, but lily-white all through, and without stain or flaw. Some people are almost like that; the more we look into them, the holier they seem. Alas! that such should be so rare. Then, too, the alabaster vase was closed up at the neck, so that none of its goodness could come out. Many hearts lie open to the light and air, and the odour of what is within them comes steaming up to all men's nostrils. Let us not blame them, but let us remember that there are others whose goodness we can never really know till death comes and shatters the frail body, and the house—the whole world as it were—is filled with the odour of the ointment. Who would have known what St. Stephen was if he had not been persecuted? The stones that broke and crushed the pure vessel of his body, let loose the fragrance of his soul which ascended to heaven with those beautiful words, " Lord, lay not this sin to their charge. Lord Jesus, receive my spirit." We have perhaps some St. Stephens now among us—alabaster vases closed up, but ready when the call comes to be broken to pieces for Christ, and pour out the whole treasure of their hidden sweets before him. Now and then we hear of such; brave soldiers, faithful missionaries, devoted clergymen, unselfish nurses, generous rich men who give their all to Christ—aye, and poor people too, and even little children, who sacrifice their time, their strength, their pleasure, and what is hardest of all, their own will and wishes for His sake. Of such we can only say, may God grant us, at however humble a distance, to follow in their footsteps! If we cannot be like

the pure alabaster vase of ointment, or the
precious cup of wine, if we are only plain
brown earthenware, yet let us endeavour to do
what we can in the calling to which we are
called, remembering that of him who gives only
a cup of cold water in the service of Christ, we
are told, "Verily I say unto you, he shall in no
wise lose his reward."

XIII.

A CROWN.

As we look out of the window we notice some one going by whistling a tune—a baker's boy in a white jacket, with a tray full of cakes, hot out of the oven, on his head. You would not, perhaps, think there was much to be said about him ; and he, probably, if you offered him "a penny for his thoughts," would have but a very poor little pennyworth to give you. He is just like any other boy we see in the streets.

"Well, then," perhaps you say, "why did you touch my arm and ask me to notice him ?" To tell you the truth, because I never can see a man carrying loaves on his head in that way without going back in thought many thousand years, and many, many hundred miles away.

The place, as perhaps you will guess, is the land of Egypt ; the time, when Joseph was in prison interpreting the dreams of Pharaoh's servants. You remember in the fortieth chapter of Genesis how Pharaoh's chief butler (or cup-bearer) and chief baker were both in prison, and how, after the chief butler had told his dream, the chief baker told his. " Behold, I had three white baskets on my head, and in the uppermost basket there was of all manner of bake-meats for Pharaoh, and the birds did eat them out of the basket upon my head." And you will remember what a fatal interpretation Joseph gave to this dream. On this we cannot now dwell, instructive as it is. What we desire to notice at present is the way in which some of our commonest habits and customs may be traced to very early times ; and this particular custom of carrying burdens on the head, will suggest a good deal to us if we give our minds to it.

There is nothing more delightful when one is —say at some little seaport town in the North of England—than to watch the fishermen's wives walking about, often on very rough ground, or up steep flights of steps, with a bucket of water or a laden basket on their heads. Queens and princesses might envy that dignified, steady, even walk and that perfect balance. There is a stateliness about these women that makes the poor rough wooden vessel look like a royal crown, so gracefully do they carry it, without ever raising

K

a finger to keep it in its place, their hands busy all the while with a heavy piece of blue knitting —a coarse jersey, which will keep brother, husband, or son, warm in the storms on some cold, wet, blusterous night at sea. And it is, I believe, a well-known fact, that in all countries where the women walk with the greatest majesty and grace, they have learnt it from carrying some kind of burden on the head. The ancients, who were always on the look-out for everything beautiful, caught up this idea. You may see it still in some of their buildings, or imitations of them in this country. A stone pillar, support-ing the roof of the temple, and made like a finely-formed, graceful woman, clothed from head to foot in a garment which veils but does not hide the beauty of the limbs underneath, and who stands steadfastly with a bushel-measure on her head. Is it a burden, or a crown ? It is a crown, for it is a glory to her; she is not ashamed of work. And yet it is a burden ; for who can wear a crown without feeling its weight ?

This was, no doubt, what the stone-cutter felt when he made this royal figure of a working woman. He wanted to teach us all that there is no reason to blush at being seen carrying

heavy loads and doing hard labour. Our very
work itself is a crown. What we may well be
ashamed of is having *no* burdens to bear, taking
no trouble, going about the world bare-headed
and empty-handed. Let us think of this. when
we are disposed to look down. on others, or to
fancy others will look down on us, for bearing
the burden and heat of the day.

Here comes a poor girl from the harvest field,
with her gleanings on her head. That is *her*
crown. Heavy as it is, she would not wish it
lighter. Here is an old woman with her bundle
of sticks. Tired as she is, we give her joy;
That load is *her* crown. Here is an Italian image-
boy, with his stand of pretty plaster figures on
his head. That is *his* crown. It is heavy, and
yet far more honourable to him than if he idled
about doing nothing. And other labourers in
turn pass by us, hard-working people, all crowned
inwardly if not outwardly. For some burdens
in these days are borne outside the head, but
many, many more are carried about within it.

Then, on the other hand, there are some other
people whom, perhaps, we may at first be
tempted to envy. Here is a beautiful young
bride, all in white, with her crown of orange-
blossoms and her fine lace veil. Who would not

wish to be in her place ? So fair, so admired, so beloved, so rich, perhaps so happy. But she and we are both mistaken, if we think that crown, elegant and graceful as it is, does not bring its load of duty, aye, and its burden of care, with it. The light-hearted girl, the playful creature that danced and sang, and seemed never to have known trouble and sorrow, will soon be the thoughtful mistress of a house, the careful wife, and perhaps the anxious mother. If she is wise, she takes her share of the work of life willingly, thankfully, and joyously. If she remembers that her crown implies a burden, her burden will sooner or later become a crown, for which she is to be honoured and cherished.

Here, again, is a king, sitting on his corona-tion chair. The archbishop places the crown of the realm on his anointed head. The people shout " God save the King." The nobles do obeisance to him. Every one thinks how beauti-ful the crown is with its red velvet and gold, and flashing, dazzling, circlet of precious stones. Hardly anyone, except the king himself, knows how heavy it is, how tiring to the brows of the wearer.

But what is the weight of the crown on the king's *head* compared with the burden of royalty in his *heart?* Day and night that load is there. The golden crown, with its velvet and diamonds, may be taken back to the State jewel-house— put away once more in the coffer which held it, locked up with triple bolts. But the burden *never* goes. The care of a great and populous nation, of peace and war, of Church and State, of law and justice, of commerce and merchandize, of the prosperous and of the poor, is always on the king's heart. Only death can take away that burden.*

And as with kings, so with all other rulers and great men. The duke's coronet, the plumed helmet of the brave general, the judge's wig, and the bishop's mitre, all mean, not only honour,

---

* Some readers here will perhaps think of the noble lines on this subject in Shakspere's Henry IV., Part II, Act iv, Scene 4, and the still grander burst in Henry V., Act iv, Scene 1 :—

"Upon the king!—let us our lives, our souls,
Our debts, our careful wives, our children, and
Our sins, lay on the king. He must bear all."

And they may possibly read with interest the words addressed by another King of England (James I.) to his eldest son, whom he looked on as his probable successor: "Consider, that being born to be a king, ye are rather born to *onus* [burden] than *honos* [honour] not excelling all your people so far in rank and honour, as in daily care and hazardous painstaking for the dutiful administration of that great office that God hath laid upon your shoulders."

but the burden of care which goes with honour, and for which the great are honoured.

If those who grudge at the greatness of others only knew at what a price it is purchased, and how heavy all these crowns are, they would often be silent, instead of complaining about what they cannot understand, and murmuring against those set over them, as the Israelites did against Moses and Aaron.

So in the natural world. The blade of corn has its crown, the beautiful heavy-hanging ripened ear. The orchard tree has its crown, rich red and golden apples, at once its glory and its burden. And yet all these gifts are not for the bearer's own sake, but for that of others. What is the ear of wheat for, except to be reaped and made into bread? What is the fruit for, but to be plucked and eaten? So too, the poor boy we spoke of at first, does not wear his crown, if we may call it so, for himself. Nor does the poor woman with her heavy bundle on her head. Some one else is to profit by their labours. So with the king's crown. He wears it for the sake of others. So with us all, who may receive some crown of praise or thanks for our work. Let us say to ourselves, "This talent, this gift, this office, was not given to me for my own glory, but for the good of others. I am only like an apple-tree bearing apples for others to gather, an ear of wheat growing that others may be fed, a boy or girl carrying something on my head that may benefit someone else." If we once thought of that, there would be little room for pride and vanity left in any of our hearts, only of thankfulness to God, the giver of all good things, and a hearty desire and prayer to do our very best, to bring forth fruit abundantly, to enrich others with our stores, and to be good stewards of whatever God has placed under our care. The greater the burden on the head, the broader the shadow it casts, and the less do we see of the face of him who carries it. So "the world knows nothing of its greatest men."

You will, doubtless, have thought of something besides this. There is one crown we read of—the only one our Lord wore upon earth. You will all remember that it was a crown of thorns. But unless we go back to the early Bible history the fulness of what was thereby meant does not appear.

We read in the third chapter of Genesis, that after the Fall, God said to Adam, " Cursed is the ground for thy sake ; in sorrow shalt thou eat of it all the days of thy life. Thorns also and thistles shall it bring forth to thee ; and thou shalt eat the herb of the field.   In the sweat of thy face shalt thou eat bread, till thou return unto the ground ; for out of it wast thou taken : for dust thou art, and unto dust shalt thou return."

Here we see the origin of our labour and toil. It was God's curse for man's sin ; and the thorns and thistles remind us of that curse.   And yet we know that labour is a blessed and honourable thing.   A great poet speaks of God's love as—

> " Turning the thistles of a curse
> To types beneficent."

By this he meant to say that the very thorns which were to be the source of so much pain and labour to man, and over which the sweat of his brow was to fall, and bedew the earth whence he was taken, were to be hallowed and glorified by being twined about the divine brow of our dying Saviour, our ever living King, whose sweat that night before His passion was like great drops of blood falling down to the ground.

Think of that, hard-working men and women, on whose heads the burden of care and toil is ever pressing, whose foreheads are moist with travail and weariness, who are for ever struggling with the thorns and thistles of this barren bewildering world. Who would shrink from that curse which Christ has turned into a blessing? Who would ever be ashamed of labour, when He bore the crown of labour upon the cross? Who would ever grudge any pain, any trouble, any shame for Him who took it all on Himself for man? Happy are they whom He has called to the fellowship of His sufferings!

You too, will assuredly think of this, great men, high-born women, all you who are crowned in the eyes of the world, either by your noble birth, your exalted station, or your extraordinary talents or gifts. Your crown is a burden; perhaps you say it yourselves. You feel the load of care and responsibility, of having to be answerable for so many others, who in some way look up to you and depend on you.

But what are your burdens to those which Christ bore for us all? Fathers and mothers again, *you* have a crown. Your children are your crown. But with that crown, as with all crowns comes the burden of duty, and the care for the souls of others.

Where then must we all look? Think of the weight of that crown of thorns. It was a light thing in the hand, but O, how unspeakably insupportably heavy on the brows. For what did it stand for? Adam's curse. The guilt of all Adam's sons and daughters. Jesus Christ was like a solitary pillar on whose head rested the burden of the universe. He was like the scape-goat on whose head the high priest on the day of atonement confessed the sins of the whole house of Israel.

"The Lord hath laid on him the iniquity of us all." O kings and princes, O councillors and wise men, O anxious heavy-laden souls, what are *your* burdens compared with His? What crown ever pressed so heavily as that crown of thorns? To whom should you take your load of care but to Him who bore our sin and sorrow on the cross?

We are told of a brave warrior of old who overcame the infidels in the Holy Land, and whom his comrades proposed, as a reward, to crown king of Jerusalem.* "No," said he, "It is not for me to wear a diadem of gold where my Saviour was crowned with thorns." Let us think of him if we are ever tempted to vain glory. The crown of thorns is the only one fit for us. Thorns of labour, thorns of pain, thorns of repentance. If we would seek any other lot in this life, we shall not be followers of Christ.

* Godfrey de Bouillon.

And yet there is one other crown the Bible tells us of—the crown of victory. "They do it," says St. Paul, speaking of those who win a race, "to obtain a corruptible crown, but we an incorruptible." Not a fading wreath, but one that never fades. For all true labour, for all patient suffering, for all constant faith, there is we know a crown laid up in heaven. "Henceforth," says St. Paul, "there is laid up for me a crown of righteousness." "When the chief shepherd shall appear," says St. Peter, "ye shall receive a crown of glory that fadeth not away." "Be thou faithful unto death," says our Lord by St. John, "and I will give thee a crown of life."

But how will the saints wear those crowns? vain-gloriously, self-righteously? As if they were of their own winning and deserving? Heaven forbid! All they have, all they are, all they hope for, is from God. "They cast their crowns down before the throne, and worship Him that liveth for ever and ever, saying, Thou art worthy, O Lord, to receive glory, and honour, and power, for thou hast created all things, and for Thy pleasure they are, and were created."

May God give us grace so to bear every burden here, the weight of labour, the weight of pain, the weight of care, aye, and the weight of earthly honour, if such be our lot, that we may, through the merits of Him who wore the crown of thorns for us, be fitted to cast our heavenly crowns hereafter before his resplendent and all-glorious throne!

XIV.

A THOUGHT FOR CHRISTMAS.

THIS MAY BE FOUND SUITABLE FOR HOSPITALS.

"Emmanuel, God with us."

"AND they heard the voice of the Lord God walking in the garden in the cool of the day, and Adam and his wife hid themselves from the presence of the Lord." Now, how are we to reconcile these two things? How is that "Emmanuel, God with us," should be, as it were, the brightest jewel in the crown of gospel promise; and yet that every one of us should enter so fully into that feeling of Adam and Eve? How often have we wished to do as they did—to hide even from one another? There is, it seems, something in us that cannot bear to be watched even at times when we are aware of no particular desire to do wrong, or of having done anything specially wicked. To be followed about by the eye of another drives us almost mad, though we may feel it is foolish to shrink from it so much.

Some of you have, perhaps, read the account of that poor queen of France, Marie Antoinette, who was dethroned and afterwards beheaded in the dreadful revolution.   In the last months of her life she was shut up in prison alone ; and yet not alone, for there were guards always watching her.   She could not rise or lie down, dress herself, say her prayers, work or be idle, weep or be silent, but a soldier's eye was upon her.   Can we imagine anything more annoying and fretting to a wounded spirit such as hers?

And not long ago there was an account (which perhaps you may have seen) of a French school, in which the boys were always watched. At their tasks, in their playground, there was always some one looking on ; at night a lamp was kept burning in the long gallery, and some one was constantly stationed there.   They were never, as we say, "to themselves."   And a curious thing happened.   The master discovered in the playground, a sort of little dark hole under the earth, and some half-a-dozen boys crowded into it.   It was, I believe, too low for them to stand up, and too dark for them to do anything.   Then, you will say, "What could have been the pleasure of being there at all?" Simply because there they were out of sight.

There they were relieved for a few moments from the distress of being under the eye of their master ; not that they were particularly naughty boys, but they had in them that instinct, which we all have, of hating to be watched.

Now, why should this feeling be so strong in us all? It is because we are fallen creatures, and carry about with us a miserable sense of perpetually falling short of what we know we ought to be, and think others will expect of us. In mere outside appearance, how far do we, for the most part, come short of the beauty, and health, and grace, which we should like the world to see in us. And our souls are no less faulty in this respect than our bodies ; they will not bear severe scrutiny. We cannot imagine an angel shrinking from being looked upon, however closely. The brighter the light shone on his lustrous wings, his pure and beautiful members, his noble and unwrinkled brow, the more glory it would disclose. And yet such is the majesty of God's presence, that before Him the very angels veil their faces. How much more then must *we* shrink, and that, not only from the eye of God, but from the gaze of fallen beings like ourselves ?

We have a miserable sense of spiritual

deformity, and hence we are for ever seeking to hide, as Adam did, among the trees of the garden. We may sometimes succeed perhaps in deceiving our fellow men. But do what we will we cannot get away from Almighty God. All the leaves of the garden will not shelter us from His piercing sunshine. God *is* with us. "If I climb up into heaven, thou art there; if I go down to hell, thou art there also. If I say, peradventure the darkness shall cover me, then shall my night be turned into day. Darkness and light to thee are both alike."

Now you will say, "This is nothing new. I have heard it over and over again, even from childhood." Doubtless, and so have we all. But do we live as if we had? Or do we not, men, women, and children alike, require to be perpetually reminded of it? Some may deny that God is present everywhere, and knows everything. A far larger number merely put it out of their minds and do not allow themselves to dwell upon it. But what does the Bible say? "The wicked shall be turned into hell, and all the people that forget God." Should we live as we do if this great truth of God's presence were always in our minds? Would Cain have killed Abel if *he* had thought of it? Should we laugh at holy things if we believed that the Holy One really heard us ? Should we be so hard on one another as we are, if we thought God noticed our harshness ?

We may have heard stories of kings and princes going about in disguise, dressed up like beggars, and seeing how their subjects behaved themselves, and who were the really good people and who were the hypocrites ; and like many other stories that we are inclined to call childish, they have a deep moral behind them.

Here we are, perhaps, a large party in this room. Fancy how we should feel if that person in the corner were to get up and turn out to be the Duke of So-and-so, or one of Her Majesty's Ministers, or of the Royal Family. I fear the first thing we should think of would be, " Dear ! if I had known *that*, I would not have said such and such things. I'm sure I wouldn't have let him see me so out of temper, or hear me using such bad words, or telling tales, or see me behaving in such a low unbecoming way." This would be the first feeling, the next, of still greater shame that such a thing should make any difference to us.

For, only think, the King of Kings—One greater than the greatest, IS here. His ear is wounded

L

by every bad word; He is of purer eyes than to behold iniquity; He suffers with those we cause to suffer, and says to us as He did to Saul, "Why persecutest thou ME?" And at the last day he will tear off all our disguises; call us forth from the cool and pleasant shade of our fruitful and flowery garden trees, and say to us, as to Adam of old, "Hast thou eaten of the forbidden fruit? hast thou disobeyed ME?" O, what if the curse should come afterwards— not as upon Adam, a curse for all time, but a curse for ever and ever, for all eternity. How are we to escape it? Is there any hope of pardon left for us?

Let us look at the other side: "They shall call his name Emmanuel, God with us." And this is to be a comfort to us! How? That dreadful and terrible God whom we sought to avoid, will *He* be with us? Yes indeed—with us in His love, with us in His mercy, with us in His sympathy or fellow-feeling.

You must have known what it is to have "with you" those whom you care about. It is not that you want to talk to them, though that may be delightful; it is not that they may wait upon you, or do things for you; it is simply the sense of their being there. I knew an old woman once who had been left a widow, and she hung her husband's old coat over the back of his arm-chair, where she could always see it, because, she said, it made it almost seem as if John (that was his name) was still with her. Now what *can* an old coat hanging over the back of a chair do for any one? Of what use can it be for a little child, who is frightened at being in the dark, to feel there is some one alive and awake in the room with him? What good is it to a sick man to have his wife sit by him when she can do nothing perhaps but look at him? Why should he go to sleep so much more easy if he has hold of her hand? Why do so many of us when we are going anywhere, beg some one or other to go with us, not that we in any way expect to need their help, but only "for company?"

Whether we can give a reason for it or not, we all agree in acknowledging that such is our feeling. Still more do we care to have "with us" those friends who *can* protect us, *can* help us, *can* advise and support us. Who then is our best Friend? the friend who is never unjustly angry, who has no wish or will but for our good, who is far, far more patient with us than we are with one another, who knows all the troubles

L 2

that we cannot put into words, all the wishes that we hardly dare to frame? Surely you will all answer, Our Lord Jesus Christ, Emmanuel, God with us. The Friend that sticketh closer than a brother, will He be with us? Yes, indeed. "In all their afflictions He was afflicted, and the angel of His presence saved them." He says, "When thou passest through the waters I will be with thee, and through the rivers they shall not overflow thee; when thou walkest through the fire thou shalt not be burned, neither shall the flame kindle upon thee:" Isaiah xliii, 2.

Christmas is here, with its snow, and its cold, and its privations. It was to such a bare and bitter world that the loving Saviour came. Poverty is here with its sharp cares and small every-day trials. He was rich, yet for our sakes He became poor, that we through His poverty might be rich. Pain is here—wakeful nights, sickening hearts, suffering bodies; and Christ hath also suffered for us. He said, "My soul is exceeding sorrowful, even unto death; tarry ye here, and watch with me." Sin and Satan are here, enticing and threatening us by turns. And Christ was in all points tempted like as we are—yet without sin.

Death is here hovering about us, shaking his dart triumphantly over us; delaying awhile, it may be, to strike that blow which must and will come to one and all, and perhaps first to him who looks for it least. But Christ has tasted death for all, and taken away the bitterness of death for those who love and serve Him, and prepared for them a happy home in eternal life. Only let us remember this. If we want to be with God then, we must have God with us now, and we must try to live always as if we knew He were watching us. Not as a guard, bending on his prisoners hard and unfriendly eyes; not as a master, threatening his slaves; but as our best Friend, our noblest Example, our tender Father, our most loving Saviour.

With us in prayer, with us at the Lord's table, with us at the marriage altar, with our children at the baptismal font, with us in joy, with us in sorrow, with us at our work, with us in our pleasure-taking (ah! how we need to think of Him then;) with us in our sick beds, and in the hour of death, when our hands are growing so cold that no human touch can warm them, and our cheeks so rigid that the kisses of husband or wife, child or friend, are no longer felt by them; then, O my God, be Thou with us all! Leave us not, neither forsake us, O God of our salvation. Let us feel Thine everlasting arms beneath us. Let our trust be under the shadow of Thy wings. Grant us, one and all, to behold Thy presence in righteousness; to be satisfied, when we awake, with Thy likeness.

FLETCHER AND SON, PRINTERS, NORWICH.

Milton Keynes UK
Ingram Content Group UK Ltd.
UKHW040139160224
437928UK00003B/38

9 783385 251298